SMALL TOWN KING

MARION MEADOWS

This is a work of fiction. All characters and events in this novel are drawn from the author's imagination and used fictitiously. Any resemblance to real events or persons is entirely coincidental.

Created with Vellum

CONTENT WARNING

This book deals with adult themes about race and gender that some may find potentially offensive.

It also contains potentially triggering scenes.

While a love story, Small Town King aims to stay true to the spirit of its setting. Some readers may find certain content and language objectionable. This book is about a steamy and controversial romance. Please be advised. -MM

DESCRIPTION

A segregated small town forbids interracial love...

And Roman McCall wants to keep it that way.
Handsome, rich, and powerful, his word is law on the mountain.
In public, he's a tyrant.
In private? Temptation rules.

Young single mother Serena Jones is in big trouble.
She worked her butt off to provide for her son and live an honest life.

When the powerful McCall family sets out to ruin her, only the King can help.
But he demands a chilling price: her body, whenever he wants.

Serena knows Roman is a monster with a stone heart.
But could this ruthless man be more than he seems?
Or is she trapped in a dangerous game with no escape?

The people that walked in darkness have seen a great light : they that dwell in the land of the shadow of death, upon them hath the light shined.

— ISAIAH 9:2

CHAPTER 1
PIKE HILL

"Ma, somebody's outside the house."

Serena Jones looked up from the pot of grits bubbling on the stove. Her hand froze mid-reach to the butter. "What did you say, baby?"

"There's a man outside," repeated six-year-old Isaiah. "It's Curley!"

Serena turned off the stove.

"Go to the room and lock the door. And don't come out no matter what you hear."

"Don't let him in," Isaiah urged, his face tensing in fear.

"It's okay baby," said Serena, herding Isaiah quickly to her bedroom. She tried to sound calm as she could be. "Just don't make a sound. Don't leave this room. No matter what, you hear me?"

Isaiah looked ready to cry, but he already knew crying was no use.

"Lock that door," his mother reminded him, backing out of the room and shutting the flimsy piece of wood that offered the only defense between her helpless child and the bastard hollering out front.

"Serena!"

Don't let him inside. Don't let him see Isaiah.

Once she heard Isaiah turn the latch, she moved to the front door and opened it quickly, grabbing the first thing she could lay hands on— the pot of grits.

"What the hell do you want?" She shouted.

Curley McCall leaned against the door of his Hurricane and crossed one cowboy boot over the other. Sunlight glinted off his silver spurs. "I reckon the same thing I had last time," he sneered.

"Just stay away from me, Curley. I'll burn your damn eyes out."

"With cold grits? I don't think so." Casually Curley took out his gun and pointed it at her head. "Drop it."

Her hands clenched tighter around the handle.

Curley leveled the gun at her breasts. His eyes were flat and cold, the eyes of a snake. Then he moved the barrel sideways and fired it directly through the house.

With a scream she dropped the pot; cold grits exploded in all directions, splattering over her legs. She tried to dart back inside, but he was faster.

"Isaiah! Curley, no... Please..."

The bones in her wrists ground together as Curley wrenched her arm behind her back and stepped closer, kicking aside the pot. He pressed her into the front door, grinding his crotch against her ass.

"See?" he said, his breath smelling like sour whiskey. "You can play nice with me, sugar. I just want you to play nice."

He grabbed her hand and forced it at an extreme angle to press between his legs. Her stiff fingers grasped only softness. For a horrible moment Serena believed she felt it harden, but the moment passed, and Curley gave a groan of frustration. It served him right. Ever since the terrible night he'd forced himself on Serena, his man's part had remained limp as a worm.

Curley dug his hips into her so hard she felt his pelvic bone. "Fix it, you rotten little bitch," he panted. "I know you can fix it." He put the gun on the railing to work off his belt buckle.

She squeezed him with all her strength.

He broke away in a howl of pain and Serena dropped, her hand closing on the cooking pot's handle. As he scrambled for the pistol Serena brought the pan up in a short arc that hit the bone of Curley's wrist dead center.

Next time get a knife, idiot!

Just barely she avoided his clutches, darted inside and slammed the deadbolt home. Holes opened up in the trailer's siding as Curley fired carelessly at the house. She crawled to Isaiah's room on her hands and knees.

"Isie? You okay?"

“Yes, Ma,” came the terrified reply through the door. “I laid down like you told me.”

The bloated floor of the trailer trembled as another truck came rumbling up the holler. Serena heard a new voice shouting. Curley shouting back. There were footsteps, and someone pounded on her door.

“Sarie? You in there?” came a man’s quavering voice.

Jessomy.

The third brother.

Serena didn’t say a word. With these McCalls, one devil was bad as another. Especially the ones that smiled in your face. She buried her head in her hands, wondering if the nightmare would ever end. Curley picked up an old chair from the yard and sent it right into her front window. The glass cracked from side to side but didn’t give him the satisfying explosion he was looking for.

“Fucking bitch!” He roared. “I’ll be back, you little cunt.” His Hurricane pulled away in a belch of smoke.

But the ordeal was not over. Jessomy pounded and pounded on the door, begging her to come out. “He’s gone, Serena. See? You’re safe now.”

“Go away!”

“Sarie, come out. Just come out.”

I wish I had a gun.

Finally he got the picture and left. Serena took a moment to collect herself before she opened the bedroom door. Isaiah nearly knocked her flat. He didn't cry, he just shook all over like a tiny tree in a storm and hugged her hard.

"Is he gone?"

"Yes, baby."

"Your face is messed up."

"It's worse than it looks."

"Why can't we move, Ma?"

"We just can't. Not yet."

"Why?"

We got nowhere to go. That's why.

"I miss Pa."

Isaiah had never said so before. "Pa was a bad man," she reminded him. "He hurt me bad. You were little so you don't remember. It's okay to miss him, but I don't."

"Curley is worse."

"Maybe." Serena stroked his hair. "Isie, I'll figure out what to do. We can leave here soon, okay?"

Isaiah nodded. He was a forgiving and loving child. Serena wondered when he would stop believing her lies. She hugged her son tighter, trying not to cry. "You hungry? I'll make you some grits."

She went with no dinner that night. Isaiah slept in her arms. She let him go only to put a bucket under the leaking roof when a rainstorm blew in. Settling back down, mentally she counted out the money she had left from selling candies. It was nowhere near enough to escape or even keep the lights on. You could barely feed a roach on that money. She might be better off surrendering Isaiah to the State and making her way down to the valley. But the thought of losing her son was unthinkable. She'd sooner lose her life.

"Ma?" Isaiah said sleepily. "Don't cry."

I'm sorry. I'm trying, baby.

"I'm not crying. There's just something in my eye."

"Okay."

"Goodnight, Isaiah. Tomorrow will be better. We'll do something fun."

"Okay, Ma."

"I love you."

"Love you, Ma."

In the dark, Serena prayed the same prayer she'd been praying all her life.

It went like this:

God, please get me out of here. I'll do anything if you just get me out.

CHAPTER 2

BUBBA'S WHORE

"It ain't right," whined Jessomy McCall. "It just ain't right."

"What ain't right?" rasped his cousin Roman, idly twirling a pen on his desk. Roman had always thought the youngest brother of Curley and Bubba to be a bit of a soft biscuit. He hoped this wouldn't prove to be a waste of time, but it was already off to a rough start.

"It ain't right," began Jessomy, tossing himself into the empty seat across from Roman. He nearly made the mistake of putting his boots on the matching chair, but a dark look from his older cousin saved his hide just in time and saved the oxblood leather from a helping of wet dirt.

"It ain't right," elaborated Jessomy.

Roman's eye moved from the clock to the mountain of work littered across his desk.

"Roman, the thing is, it's a bit of a long story."

"You might as well tell it, since you took the trouble to be here."

"Well, sir, remember how your brother killed my brother Bubba?"

"Bubba shot himself in the heart by accident," corrected Roman coldly. This was the coroner's official story. Being a firsthand witness to the crime himself, Roman knew it was a lie, but he also knew a lie repeated often enough became the truth.

"Your brother Bubba what?" Roman prompted, before Jessomy could contradict him.

Jessomy frowned. "My brother Bubba – who died – well, he had this woman–"

"Hold on," said Roman, throwing up a hand. "Let me just stop you there. I don't handle man-woman stuff." He'd been down this road before with family members. Many times.

"Roman. I just can't leave until I tell you what I come to tell you," Jessomy insisted with uncharacteristic bullishness. "I'm fit to be tied about the whole dang thing."

"Then hurry up and tell it."

"Well, a few years back Bubba was out in some holler down in the negro side," said Jessomy. "He got to drinking with this man named Rayvaughn. Ray was the darkie with the golden tooth. Dirty Ray, we called him."

"I remember him. Mean son of a bitch," grunted Roman.

"So while Bubba and Dirty Ray is drinking...out comes this lil' girl only fourteen years. She's Ray's niece."

Roman opened his top drawer, took out the finely aged whiskey he kept for emergencies, and fortified his coffee. He didn't offer any to Jessomy.

"Well," Jessomy continued, sadly eyeing the whiskey as it returned to its drawer, "Dirty Ray and Bubba start throwing dice, and the young thing is servin up sandwiches and applejack, and the two of them are getting drunk as bees. I'm sitting in the corner just watching, you know, 'cause I know how Bubba gets."

"Right."

"Dirty Ray starts losing at the game, and Bubba keeps winning, until there's no more money left for Ray to bet with, so he offers Bubba something else."

"The girl," said Roman wearily.

"That's right," said Jessomy. "Ray says Bubba can have her, and since she's a virgin, it's worth more. Bubba says yes."

"I see."

"Well, as I said, the girl was breeding age."

Jessomy noticed a change in Roman's demeanor, but couldn't precisely say what. Slanted black eyes stared at him coldly.

"Breeding age, as I said," Jessomy continued uneasily. "And, well, I guess Bubba got her in a condition. Some months later Dirty Ray shows up on Snatch Hill with her, and she's got a babe in arms what looks just like Bubba except maybe handsomer."

"No difficult accomplishment."

"What was that?"

"Nevermind. Go on with the story."

"Ray says he ain't taking care of no McCall brat, so the girl's got to stay with Bubba. Well, my big brother's fit to be tied, but he rustles up a trailer over on Pike Hill and starts keepin' the girl there. She been there ever since, raising Bubba's son."

"So you want me to kick her out? Pike Hill is on Snatch Hill land. You deal with it."

"Kick her out? No, sir. That ain't it." Jessomy gulped. "It's Curley, sir."

And there it was. Roman wondered when the third brother would enter the story. Curley McCall was never too far from any drama concerning Snatch Hill.

Jessomy said, "After your brother Rebel, er, allegedly shot Bubba, Curley was pissed. Especially when he learned what Bubba done before he died. Something most unexpected, was what Bubba done."

Roman's tone held a warning. "And what was that?"

"Bubba wrote a will before he died," Jessomy said hurriedly. "It's official and everything. Bubba left that little boy his trailer and 'everything inside it'. Those words exactly, sir. I had a look at the document myself, and though some of them words seemed overmuch, the signature was Bubba's. Knew it instantly."

"So if I follow you," said Roman, "Curley is upset because Bubba left his halfbreed son a shitcan on Pike Hill?"

"Aye, sir. But Curley is mad for another reason, too. The girl cursed him."

"*Cursed* him?"

"Yes. But, uh, I better let Curley tell you that part." Jessomy sniffed. "What Curley's doing to that woman ain't right, curse or no."

"And you want me to make Curley stop his reign of terror."

"Yeah," nodded Jessomy eagerly. "And if you have to kill him, I understand. I never did like the bastard."

Roman rubbed his jaw. "What does she do for work? The woman?"

"She can't work 'cause Curley's got the whole hill makin' sure she don't leave the trailer, just to torture her. She used to sell candy–Bubba would drop it off in town, if he remembered. She had the kid five years ago now, so she's about twenty years old and she's a Scorpio with a Virgo moon."

"What's her blood type?" said Roman with a touch of sarcasm.

"O positive," said Jessomy.

It was coming together now. "You want the girl for yourself, don't you, Jessomy?" Roman asked bluntly.

"I liked Serena for years, even if she was Black. And now that Bubba's dead..." Jessomy trailed off before blurting defiantly, "Well, Bible says it ain't wrong."

"Why don't you call Curley off yourself? Be the hero."

"I do sometimes...But I'm scared of him. And he's more scared of you, so I figured..." He trailed off hopefully.

Roman looked the younger man in the eye. “Has Curley been stealing from the clan, Jessomy?”

Jessomy’s mouth opened and closed like a trout. “I’m sure I don’t know nothing about that, sir,” he stammered.

“You want me to go out there and rescue your damsel, Jesso, you better start talking. Last year I found an entire shipment unaccounted for, and all signs pointed to your hill.”

“C-Curley’s skimmed some dope off the top, sure,” Jessomy confessed, squirming in the seat. “I ain’t no rat or nothing, but that’s what he’s done. Sure.”

“Where’s he running it?” Roman demanded, narrowing his eyes.

“Into West Virginia. He’s got buddies in the back hills to get it off the mountain. And that ain’t the half.” Jessomy swallowed nervously, deciding to make a clean breast of the whole thing. “He’s bringing other stuff in. Pills. He knows some fellas working at the railroad. Every time a train blows through town, they do a toss-over and Curley gets a package off the tracks. He’s got a couple trailers near the Green Trees, and that’s where he cooks the meth and presses the pills. Then he sells ‘em down in Rowanville. I reckon Duke knew about it,” Jessomy added with a touch of defensiveness, unable to forsake his clan loyalty.

“Alright,” said Roman after a thoughtful pause. “Well, thank you, Jessomy. This was very revealing.”

“You going to see Curley, sir?”

“Yes.”

"You'll tell him to leave the girl alone?"

"I'll see what I can do," said Roman shortly. Taking the hint, Jessomy scraped back from the desk and made his retreat.

After Jessomy left, Roman tapped his pen against the ledgers, his dark eyes vaguely fixed on a corner of the room.

The Snatch Hill McCalls were a branch of the family tree Roman had long desired to prune. His father entertained the grasping brood of cousins for his own reasons, but with Duke dead, and Roman's control over the clan now absolute, it was high time to bring the wayward sons to order.

They contributed nothing to the family but drama. Constantly bickering and killing each other. Turning their hill into an open sewer. The leader Bubba–now dead–had been a belligerent sot. Roman dubbed Jessomy a mere coward, but Curley McCall was a thoroughbred jackal: a coward still, but dangerous.

As for the protagonist of Jessomy's story... Roman smiled grimly to himself. Jessomy was likely exaggerating. He'd painted the girl as some helpless victim. In Roman's experience, women were never so innocent as they appeared.

Not his business. Not his problem.

An hour later Roman holstered his gun, threw on his jacket and stetson, and blazed out of his hill to the other end of Florin. As he entered the Narrows, his concentration laser-focused on the road. The Pegasus's speedometer needle inched steadily to the right, the V10 engine responding to every nudge like a blooded stallion under a cowboy's spur. He flew around the corners, weaving through mountain passes built along old mule trails. The air roared past his ears, cold and sharp and wild. Then the road widened, and deep potholes tested his shocks, sending him bumping and flying all the way into Snatch Hill. Driving got him the closest he'd ever felt to sanity.

Roman took a shortcut to the main trailer park where Curley and his goons were likely to be posted. The smell of roasting meat came thickly in the air. Roman settled himself from the blood-racing ride with a smoke. The park held about a dozen Snatch Hill families, not all of them his cousins. It was a shit hole. Piles of debris nearly blockaded the road. Festering bags of garbage, torn open by raccoons and other varmints, spread among the ragged tufts of jimsonweed. Nobody bothered to clean it. Nobody cared. As he smoked, he watched a junkie shuffle along the bulging chain-link fence, using a long stick to poke through the trash and jimsonweed for copper scrap. When the man raised his head Roman saw the sores weeping around his mouth. Sunken eyes blinked at him through a crust of yellow. Infected.

Losing his taste for the cigarette, Roman scrubbed it out on his boot and climbed out of the Pegasus. He walked straight into the park. A faded confederate flag waved in the slight breeze.

A little girl darted out. "Mister Roman!" she shrieked.

Roman ruffled her head. "Hi, Charlotte. You doin' good?"

"I'm fine! I lost a tooth! See?" She pulled her lips apart with two fingers.

He stooped down to inspect the gap. "So you did," he grinned. "Well, I'd lend you one of mine, but I need 'em all today."

She laughed. "Can I have some candy?"

"Find me Curley and you can have a whole dollar."

"Okay!" Charlotte zoomed off towards the trailers.

In short order Curley came out, looking drunk to the rafters and a little high. He was smaller than your typical McCall stock, with a patch of wild russet curls that thinned in the middle of his head. His narrow face had always reminded Roman of a weasel.

Charlotte crept behind the leader of the Snatch Hill gang, looking a little deflated. She nervously looked at Roman, who beckoned her over. He handed her a five-dollar bill folded inside a single. As she took the money in her small fist he saw the dark purple bruises on the back of her neck.

"Go inside, girl," Curley barked at her. Charlotte slunk off.

Curley stuck his thumbs into his belt and looked Roman up and down. "Well, if it ain't the big boss himself. Come in and have a drink."

Roman followed his cousin to a predictable scene. Half-naked sluts cavorted with men in the open. A circle of dazed drunks passed around a bowl leaking some noxious clear smoke. Children played among the camping chairs and old stumps like lightning bugs, seemingly oblivious.

Halfway to the offered seat–a rotted stump–a pitbull lunged at Roman. "Fuck off, fucking piece of shit," Curley snarled and booted the dog savagely in the ribs. It fled.

Roman accepted the warm Blue Ribbon handed to him and took a seat near Curley's own throne: a busted camping chair.

"So," the Snatch Hill leader said, crossing his heels, "To what do I owe the pleasure?"

"I was hearing stories about you and so I come to hear your side," replied Roman.

Curley sniffed. "You come to pick at me about some hill gossip?"

"I hear you're still picking up deliveries from the train tracks."

"You talked to Jessomy, didn't you? I'll kill that slimy rat," Curley seethed. He fumbled in his pockets for a tin of skoal. Shaking it between two fingers, he unscrewed it and packed himself a full lip. He left the open tin balanced on his knee.

"Look here, Roman," Curley said, his voice thickened from the tobacco plug pushing against his tongue. "I don't appreciate you taking Jessomy's word over mine. He's a craven bastard."

"You'll stop that little endeavor, Curley. Immediately."

Curley spat. "You owe me, you know. Your brother Rebel killed my brother Bubba. I'm liable to expect some compensation."

"I agree," said Roman. "As compensation I won't shoot you for stealing from the clan."

Curley's eyes went beady. "Alright, Roman. Alright."

"And there won't be any more business with the train tracks."

"Whatever you say."

"Glad we could clear that up."

"Ah... What else did my little brother talk to you about?" Curley demanded.

Roman stretched out his long legs, nudging aside a tuft of grass to reveal a used needle. "Some piece of cunt you're hiding on Pike Hill. Black girl," he grunted, watching his cousin closely.

Spit. Curley snorted. "Serena."

"You raped her?" said Roman bluntly.

"Just once. And then my dick never worked again." *Spit.* "Been about three years. The damned girl cursed me. I had a dream that said I got to do it with her again to resurrect it. Well, I been trying, but so's far I'm getting nowhere. Cursed, like I said."

This was rather more information than Roman cared to hear. "I hear she's got Bubba's kid," Roman said. "Is that true?"

"Yeah. My *nephew*." Curley sneered. "I shoulda drowned the halfbreed when I had the chance. Bubba left the bitch the whole trailer. Only reason I haven't gone up there and given them both a cold bullet is... well, I just told you." He shrugged. "But maybe I should just kill her. There's worse things than a limp dick."

"I guess." Roman stood up. He'd heard enough. "I'll see you around the harvest, Curley. I expect my dope to be accounted for. If not, I might just take it off your hide. You get me?"

Curley flushed. "One day, Roman McCall, you'll pick the wrong man to fuck with."

Roman spat right into Curley's open tin of Skoal. The tin tumbled off the smaller man's knee and splattered in the grass. Curley jerked back with a cry of surprise. Another Snatch Hill who witnessed it burst out laughing. Hands in his pockets, Roman strolled out of the park.

Part of leading the McCall family meant becoming a consistent visible presence across every hill and holler. His father excelled at that. But Roman had always been a lone wolf. As Duke's right-hand man he learned to walk unseen and appear to be nowhere.

Instead of heading to the nearest honky-tonk and getting drunk with the Bailey brothers, as he'd intended to end his evening, he went against his own judgment and decided to look in on this Serena woman.

He didn't like it. The whole thing stank.

But when Roman had a gut instinct, he followed it.

He parked at the old farmhouse on Warbler Road and made his way up to the neighboring Pike Hill on foot— an hour's walk. Roman knew almost every path and trail in Florin like the back of his hand. He could see in the dark like a cat. As the moon rose, he followed the deeply overgrown path up through a grove of poplar trees until the dark figure of a trailer took shape.

It was a small, sunken place. He circled the building, wondering if he'd come to the right spot. Instinct told him he had. Over the hum of crickets and cicadas, the wind brought the sound of a woman's voice.

Roman moved closer, drawn not only to the sound but to the glowing light of a gas lamp through the open window. Did the woman have no electricity?

He paused just outside the window, pressing his back against the siding of the trailer.

"Come on, Isaiah. I got to wash up before it gets too late."

"But it's dark, Ma." Came the child's reply. "Please don't go out."

"Isaiah, you want me to stink up the whole house tomorrow? You want your Mama stinking like old cheese? That what you want?"

Her attempt at humor failed. "No," conceded Isaiah. "But what if *he's* out there? Curley?"

"He's not. Isaiah, come on. I'm being serious now. I'll sing so you know I'm okay, alright? But I got to go. I'll be right outside."

The light turned off. Roman glanced to his right and saw a standpipe and a bucket in kicking distance. Walking lightly, he retreated for the treeline.

In a few minutes, Serena came out of the house and walked to the standpipe. She set down a cake of soap on a plate then reached behind her head and tugged at something. Her hair fanned out like the petals of a sunflower. She removed her clothes.

Serena stripped off a man's T-shirt, old jeans, panties and bra until she stood completely naked. Her dark skin was the color of good earth. She worked the pump of the standpipe until crystal clear water splashed in glittering drops over her long, shapely legs. She started to sing in a soft contralto.

Sit there, count your fingers...

She filled the bucket with water and poured it over her head. It must have been freezing cold, come straight from an underground spring.

What else is there to do?

Shining trails of light sluiced down her body. They outlined heavy breasts and generous hips. At twenty, the girl was in the prime of her beauty, lush and ripe as a sweet dark plum. She reached for a rag and dunked it in the water. She lathered up with the soap, singing the whole time. Lightning bugs darted past her.

I know you feel that you're through...

Roman stirred, aroused and stunned, unable to look away. He'd gone hard under his denim. By the grace of God–or the devil–the girl couldn't hear him breathing like a wild animal. She washed herself slowly and peacefully, taking her time. He figured this must be her only alone time she ever got to herself. She was going to enjoy it. The cold air on Pike Hill stole its fingers over Roman's wrist, willing him to take his hand from where it was now cupped hard on his crotch. A shaft of pleasure ran through the tip of his dick.

Who would ever know?

He pulled at his belt, hypnotized by the girl's movements. The cold water didn't seem to trouble her at all. She doused herself in it, rubbed the soap from her breasts, and then wet her hair. Her breasts would overflow his large hands. He stroked himself. He worked the rage and frustration out, imagining the girl would see him, approach him, fall to her knees...He imagined sucking the cold water off her breasts as she rode him right there in the long grass.

"Isaiah? You awake?" she said, dousing herself again with the water.

At the mention of her son Roman jerked himself back to reality and jerked his jeans back up his ass, guilt racing through his blood. *Sick. You're sick in the head.*

Meanwhile, Serena picked up her soap and rag and clothes and walked stark naked into the trailer.

Hours later, Roman was back home. He reheated the leftovers from his father's wake and trudged to his study. He pored over more accounts, correspondences from Weatherby, his lawyer, and lastly his own ledgers, but everything seemed blurry. He couldn't stop thinking about the girl.

Giving up, he took a bottle of whiskey to the couch. He drank it steadily until his eyes slammed shut. His dreams were dark and sexual and he woke up more than once at the climax of violent fantasies that left him angry, horny, and afraid of himself. Better just jerk off and get it over with.

He cupped himself. In his mind the girl leaned over him. She was just some faceless, nameless slut. Like many before her... No. No, she was sweet and soft. She was gentle. She stroked his chest, understanding what he needed. He just needed sweetness. He needed a woman who would get on her knees and make love to him with her mouth.

And that was what she did. She actually sucked his cock, taking him all the way down her throat as her hands caressed and squeezed him. *I know you're tired, aren't you?* Her husky voice. *You're tired. Let me take care of you. I'll be your woman... only yours. Whatever you need, Roman...*

His balls ached, and she squeezed them too. He felt delirious and controlled. He spilled creamy seed in her mouth, and she begged him for more. So he gave it to her. Endless jets of semen across her pretty lips, her breasts, her ass. He came until she dripped with it, bathing in her own degradation the way she bathed in the moonlight, and her hands stroked his thighs, encouraging him to keep coming...

He opened his eyes to a cold and empty room. Seed on his belly, his chest. His colossus frame convulsed, and more thick drops splashed out across his abs. It hurt.

I'm too old to be doing this shit. No closer to relief, he cleaned the filth off himself with the end of his shirt and heaved himself up. In the shower Roman scrubbed his skin raw, feeling like he'd stepped into some fresh new circle of bachelor hell.

I can't get involved.

It'll hurt the clan.

Can't be warring with Curley. Too much at stake.

Enough drama with the Rebel bullshit. Stay low.

Not your business.

Leave it alone.

Leave it, McCall.

CHAPTER 3

DEVILS AND ANGELS

Serena woke up tangled in the sheets. She'd sweat right through them. All because of a very crazy dream she absolutely could not share with Isaiah.

What did it mean?

She put a shaking hand to her throat, which hurt a little. The last time Bubba forced her to suck him off, she felt like this.

Stop cryin'. Stop wrigglin'. Open your legs...

She clamped her knees together and broke out in a cold sweat all over again. Years had passed since the last time she'd been violated. But the memories lingered in the corner of her mind, swooping in now and then to tear a piece out of her.

The dream was nothing like those memories.

A man found his way into her bedroom and covered her mouth with his large hand. Dream-Serena woke up underneath him, her heart pounding. She wasn't afraid at all. She knew what he'd come for, and she wanted the same thing. In fact, she parted her knees so he could sink his weight against her. She felt his hard penis digging into her thigh and she opened her legs wider with a desperate gasp. This was meant to happen. The dream-man smelled like the forest with a faint odor of tobacco smoke, the clean kind that came from rolled leaves. He bit her neck as he peeled the sheets from her body–she was naked–and began touching her all over.

His rough caresses turned her on. He loved on her from head to toe, just feeling her body like it was the most precious thing in the world. He rubbed the stretch marks on her stomach and ass, murmuring praises in a voice so deep she could barely understand him. Then the dream man dipped low to kiss her breasts. Oh God. Silently Serena prayed to not wake up. She dug her fingers through coarse curly hair–Mister Dream was black?–and he moved even lower, gently raising her thighs to rest on his shoulders. The tip of his thick cock nudged against her, demanding entry.

"Let me in, darling," he said in a voice like thundering rain. "Let me in where it's so wet."

She moaned. *Yes. Yes!*

"You're sensitive...I'll go slow."

Yes!!!

"Ma?"

Her eyes flew open and the dream vanished like a puff of smoke. She blinked stupidly at the bloated rafters of the trailer. *Damn it.*

"Isaiah? What you need, baby?" she sighed.

"There was a rat in my room," answered Isaiah, coming through the door. Dinosaur dragged on the ground as he crept up to Serena's bed and leaned over it anxiously.

Any remnants of sleep evacuated her mind. "A *rat*?"

"Yeah. It started fighting with another rat and the other rat killed it. And then the first rat went under my bed. There's blood everywhere, and it stinks."

"Lord have mercy," Serena said, already disgusted. She swung her feet out of bed. "Okay. Show me."

"When are we moving again?"

"Soon, baby. Soon," she lied, heading to the cleaning closet for the bucket and the mop.

The trailer was a nightmarish dump full of holes. Vermin of all kinds got in no matter what she tried. Roaches in the summer, mice in the winter, rats any time of year. She *hated* rats. Even when she lived with her nasty Uncle Rayvaughn it hadn't been bad as this. She blamed Bubba. He used to leave the garbage piling up for weeks in the yard. Sometimes he and his friends would go drinking out there and leave a whole mess for her to clean. When Serena begged him to remove the trash, he just put it off. She started walking the garbage down the hill herself but the rats took a liking to the trailer and frequently returned for warmth and entertainment. She'd have to ask Jessomy to bring a cat.

Then again, if Curley saw a cute fluffy animal lurking around, he'd likely shoot it.

I hate Curley. I hate him so much.

"Can I help?" Isaiah asked as she mixed water and vinegar in the cleaning bucket.

"No. I don't want you to get a disease."

"I want to help."

She stopped herself from replying sharply. Serena didn't demand extreme obedience from Isaiah. She needed to show him there were better ways to talk than shouting and snapping, which was all his bastard father had ever done.

"You can sit down and tell me a story," she suggested. "A story about Dinosaur."

"Okay," Isaiah said. "Once upon a time Dinosaur lived in a nasty old house. There were rats and roaches. And bats. And he couldn't eat any of them. He was hungry a lot."

"Poor Dinosaur."

"He wanted to live in a better house. So he found a magic coin and made a wish. And then Curley came and tried to take the coin away, but Dinosaur ate him and he died. Then Dinosaur went to live in the big house with his Ma, and they lived happily ever after."

"I like that story," Serena told him.

"Thank you."

"If you see any magic coins around, let me know."

Isaiah sat on his bed, lifting his legs as Serena attacked the floor with the mop. "What would you wish for?" he asked.

"A big cheesecake," she said, and Isaiah laughed.

• • •

The Pegasus idled at the foot of Pike Hill, the engine a mild disturbance in the quiet forest. Roman's fists clenched and unclenched around the steering wheel. He could still turn back. Leave Curley and Jessomy to work it out over the woman, and forget what he'd seen.

Sure, he could just do that.

Roman jerked into four-wheel drive and throttled the gas over deep pits made by rain and snowmelt. Pike Hill. Overgrown and shadowed, it seemed like the only living things that passed by here were the deer. It was just the type of desolate holler men hid their wicked deeds away in. The Pegasus plunged through the dense brush like a battering ram. Branches thudded against his windshield, attacking the truck until he broke free into the small clearing where the trailer he'd visited the night before sat quiet.

Too quiet.

Roman saw the impression of tires in the trampled grass before the tiny dwelling. He recognized the marks of Curley's Hurricane, but luckily the wretch himself was nowhere to be seen. Cutting the engine, Roman holstered his gun and got out, his size thirteen boots sinking into soft earth and rotted leaves. The morning air blew crisp and cold about his ears. He scanned the trailer in the clear light of day.

The property was nice and isolated, but untidy. A blackberry vine waged open war against one half of the single-wide. Broken furniture mounded up in the yard. A clothesline fluttered out back. There were a lot of plants growing out of weather-beaten pottery, and some flowers. Nothing untoward.

Suddenly the door opened, and a young black woman stepped out. Roman nearly missed a step. There she was. The nymph from the night before.

She stared at him, and he stared back. Even from a distance he could tell the girl was no ordinary beauty. His legs moved without thinking, and as he approached the porch a strange lightness rose in his chest.

Closer. Closer.

Like most people who met Serena for the first time, he noticed her eyes first. They were large, slanted, and the color of orange blossom honey, standing out in sharp relief against her dark brown skin. She was stunning, slender in the waist and curved like a succubus everywhere else. She looked very young.

He took off his Stetson, but the way her eyes leapt to his growing hair automatically made him replace it.

"And who are you?" she demanded.

"Roman McCall."

"You're a McCall? You don't look like one."

"Okay, sweetheart. What's your name?"

"Before I go telling you all of that, Roman McCall, I'd like to know what it is you think you're doing up here. And I ain't your sweetheart."

"Are you Curley's?"

The girl flinched. "No. No, I am not."

"I'm his cousin," Roman said in a tone of authority that clearly surprised her. He said, "I heard rumors about what all was going on here so I come to investigate. So you better stand here and answer some questions."

"Or what?" She challenged.

"Or I leave," he said.

She blinked. Roman saw the gears turning in her head. No, he judged. The girl was no fool.

"Alright, Mister McCall," she said, glancing back at the house with a small frown. "You come to help me, then?"

"Possibly."

She chewed her lower lip, her eyes not meeting his. "Curley and Bubba talked about some cousins they had. Rich folks who ran the business. You one of them?"

"I'm the one asking the questions. Now how old are you?"

"Twenty," she mumbled.

Just three years older than his teenage daughter, and at least from this first impression, Roman could tell the girl had a maturity about her that Katie would never gain if she lived to be ninety.

"Is the boy you have in there belonging to Bubba, or Curley?" he asked.

"Bubba. Isaiah's six years old."

"You had him at fourteen, then."

"That's right," she said to his knees.

"You got family you can stay with?" he demanded. "If you was to leave this place, I mean."

"If I had family to stay with, I'm sure I wouldn't still be here talking to you," the girl replied tartly.

"There's a women's shelter in Florin."

She looked at him like he was simple. "I can't go to that place."

"Why not?"

"Curley's cousin runs it."

He'd forgotten that. Roman rubbed his chin. "Jessomy said Curley won't let you leave the hill or take work. Is that true?"

Serena nodded. "That's right. But even if I got good work, I can't leave Isaiah alone up here. Somebody's got to watch him. Curley's always threatening to–to kill him." Her voice shook. She controlled it. "I don't mind working hard," she said firmly. "I want to save up money so we can leave this place. I want Isaiah to go to school and have friends. I want him to have a normal, happy childhood." As she spoke she reached up to push hair off her shoulder. Thick, dark marks ringed her wrists. Bruises. She saw him staring and quickly lowered her arm, but Roman caught her hand and turned it over, palm up. The marks went all the way to her elbow.

Her skin was dangerously soft. This close he could smell the scent of cinnamon coming from the back of her neck.

Bruises.

"Curley did that?" He snapped.

"Yeah." Her dilated pupils danced mesmerizingly at him. Roman suddenly forgot what he'd meant to say— had he meant to say anything?

"I'll kill him for this," was what came out.

She jerked her arm away, backing up towards the door. He'd frightened her.

"Maybe you should leave now."

"No, we're not done here, girl."

"My son is inside. If Curley finds out I was talkin' to you, I don't know what he'd do. I'm sorry. Goodbye, Mister McCall."

It took every ounce of Roman's willpower not to break the door off its hinges and drag her back out of the festering trailer. Instead, he circled the house quietly, stopping outside the window to (he guessed) her bedroom.

The door slammed as Serena burst into the room. Her quiet, wrenching sobs hit him like a punch to the gut. Roman was tall enough to see through the window; he watched the young woman weep into her hands as if there was no hope in the world. Her door opened and a small boy came in. He had fluffy pale brown hair and golden skin just a couple shades darker from Roman's. *Bubba's son.*

"Ma..." the boy gingerly touched her back.

She gasped, realizing her mistake, and quickly wiped her face on the yellowed bedsheets.

"I-Isaiah. I'm s-sorry. I just needed a minute..."

"He's still there, Ma. I can see his truck."

"We'll just wait for him to leave." She smiled bravely at her son, her eyes crinkling in a way that made her so much prettier, if that was even possible.

Unable to watch more, Roman stepped away from the window and went to his truck. He smoked, glaring at the trailer. Maybe he expected her to change her mind and come out again. But she didn't.

"What the fuck is wrong with you?" said his brother Rebel as Roman barreled into the garage. Roman made a beeline for the mini-fridge of beers. "Nothing," he snapped, hooking a six pac with his finger and dragging it out.

Rebel turned over the keys Roman had dumped on his worktable. His sandy eyebrows furrowed. Recent events had not improved the brothers' already-tense relationship.

"Where's Minnie?" said Roman provokingly.

"Inside," Rebel said.

"Good."

"You want to get your shit kicked in, Roman?"

"No. I want to talk."

"I'd lead with an apology, if I was you," said Rebel. "How about you're sorry for assaulting my woman, selling me out to Pa, and driving my niece off this mountain back to Tulsa?"

"I already apologized for the first part, I didn't do the second, and Katie ran off on her own thanks to you, who encouraged her to start foolin' around with that boy in the first place."

"Okay, Roman. How 'bout you take a long walk down Fuck Off Bridge until you get to Kissmyassistan?"

"Reb. I need your advice."

Rebel grumbled, "About what? Besides your fucked-up alignment?" He glanced over Roman's truck. "Your tires are good, at least." He leaned over the driver's side and sniffed. "Now that ain't good," he muttered. Unable to help himself, Rebel popped the hood and began fussing with the insides of the truck while Roman watched. "So what's your problem?" Rebel asked.

"Did you know Bubba had a son?"

Rebel straightened. Alarm crossed his face. "Pardon?"

"Bubba had some..." The word came to his lips but he couldn't say it. "He had some girl tucked away on Pike Hill. Black girl. A teenager." Roman retrieved a second can of beer, having emptied the first. "I mean, she ain't a teenager no more. She's got a kid–"

"Hold on," interrupted Rebel. "Slow down. You are tellin' me *Bubba has a mixed race son*?"

"Yeah."

"Shit." Rebel rubbed his jaw, looking haunted. He'd shot Bubba in the chest, killed him dead, and unknowingly taken away a child's father. "So where's the 'advice' part come in?"

"I want to know how you do it," said Roman.

"Do what, Roman?"

"Everybody's got two sides, Reb. Ain't that right? Devil and angel. You listen to the angel. Always have. It's what I always admired about you." The beer went down his throat like coals. "Seems like all I can do is heed the devil," said Roman.

Rebel tilted his head. "If I had to guess, Roman, I'd say you got the hots for Bubba McCall's baby mama."

Roman grimaced.

"She sounds a little young."

"She's twenty."

"And she's black?" Rebel queried.

"Yeah. She's darker than Minnie. She has these eyes– my God."

"Jesus. What's she like?"

"I ain't sure yet. She's stuck in some sick bullshit with Curley and I want to get her out. But I don't trust myself with her."

Rebel narrowed his green eyes. "So...?"

"I want her, but I shouldn't. Devil, angel. I'm asking you to help me pick the angel."

"Sounds like you already have," said Rebel.

"I'm worried about the family. They won't like it."

"You know what's funny?" said Rebel, selecting a wrench from an assortment on his worktable. "You've been dealing with our family near a decade longer than I have, and you still don't get it."

"Get what?"

Rebel pointed the wrench at him. "There ain't no pleasing a McCall. There ain't no compromisin' with a McCall. You try to make every McCall on this godforsaken mountain happy, you end up in an empty fuckin' house, miserable. Or dead."

CHAPTER 4
THE PROPOSAL

Serena stared at the tall stranger under the screen of her eyelashes. Her heart pounded so loud she could feel it in her toes. She sipped from the can of iced tea and nibbled at a slice of country bread slathered in jam and butter.

Roman brought a complete feast, some food she hadn't eaten in years: tea and fresh-baked rolls, huckleberry jam, cold cuts, cheese, and strawberries.

He apologized for scaring her the day before, then let her and Isaiah demolish the food while he ate a piece of bread and butter.

His behavior with Isaiah surprised her the most of all. As Isaiah hid behind her legs, terrified of the giant man with the serious face, Roman just spoke to the boy calmly, asking him questions. Isaiah's curiosity got the better of him and soon he replied to McCall with an eagerness she'd never seen him show to anyone. Of course, Roman McCall was light years different from anybody who ever came up to Pike Hill.

My name is Isaiah. I'm five years old. When I grow up, I want to be John Henry. My best friends are Ma and Dinosaur.

"Who is John Henry?" Roman asked.

"Just somebody from a story I told him."

"Hm," said Roman.

"I don't be entertaining men up here, McCall, if that's what you're thinking."

The memory came to Roman suddenly. "John Henry, the steel-driving man?"

"Uh-huh."

"My mother used to tell me that story." He frowned. "But as for entertaining men? Well, you're a young woman and you ain't ill-favored. Wouldn't be surprising."

"I've had enough of men."

"You're a little young to be saying that." Roman rubbed a thumb over his knuckles. His hands were *gigantic.*

"The only man I need in my life is my son." A man with hands like that didn't fear hard work. Or violence.

She shifted on the porch, leaning down to scratch a mosquito bite. Serena wore cutoff shorts and an old T-shirt, her natural hair held back with clips. All her clothes were old; she got them from the church drives. But she might have been wearing six-inch heels the way the tall man's gaze lingered on her calves. She tucked her feet back, self-conscious of her chipped nail polish.

After the disastrous first encounter, Serena fully expected to never see Roman McCall again. She'd cried like a baby, ashamed that he'd seen her marks. And she also cried because she realized in that moment she'd actually lost hope long ago. She didn't believe help was truly coming for her and Isaiah. It would kill her to be disappointed once again. No; easier to think Roman was just another wicked man coming to abuse her.

But now she was all cool composure. She sat calmly with Roman on her porch as if she hadn't embarrassed herself just yesterday by slamming the door in his face. But what did he want now? He seemed nearly as nervous as she was.

"I'd like to make you an offer, Serena," he said in his deep voice.

"What kind of offer?"

"One of a private nature."

Isaiah hung upside-down from the tire swing, his shirt falling over his head.

A private nature.

"I see," she whispered.

"It would be like a job. I would pay you very well."

"Alright."

"I'm a busy man, you see." Roman said. "I got wheels turning all the time. Shit to manage. Look after. But I'm still a man... When I come home on a night, I'd like a hot meal, somebody to talk to." His voice roughened. "A woman in my bed."

"A man like you can have anybody else on this mountain," she said, finding it hard to breathe. "Good lookin', rich... Mister, you don't want nothing to do with me."

"You're wrong." He rubbed the loose thread now, back and forth.

She swallowed hard.

"I would take care of you. I would never humiliate you or make you do shameful things. I'm a clean man, I ain't diseased, and bedding strange ass ain't a habit of mine. As long as you're living with me, I'd be committed to you." He took a breath. "And I'd like to provide for your son. He's a McCall, and my kin. I'd protect you both from Curley. You have my word."

"I don't know what to say."

He nodded. "You can ask me questions."

"How much?" she dared.

"Two grand a week."

She thought she hadn't heard him right. She couldn't have heard him right. That was crazy talk.

"The money is no issue to me," he said calmly. "If you need anything else for the boy, I will provide it."

Serena realized she was wringing her hands and forced herself to stop. "Well, now you've made me an offer I don't know I can refuse."

"Then don't refuse it."

"I have to think of Isaiah's wellbeing. What kind of Mama would I be running off with a stranger I barely know? You could hurt him."

"You two will stay in my guest house. It's got three bedrooms and the locks use a number code. I'll never enter without your permission."

This seemed extremely generous. Too good to be true, in fact.

Roman said, "And, if you'll consider it, I can get a woman to watch your boy. Mrs. Loving. She's looked after dozens of children in our family. Including me."

"I'd have to meet her."

"I understand." He cleared his throat. "You'll have a place to stay. A safe, clean place, with square meals. You do your duty to me, and the rest of your time is yours. In September Isaiah will go to school. I'll pay for what he needs separately even after our arrangement ends. Your boy is a McCall, and I can't have Curley threatening him." He paused again. "I intend to deal with Curley soon, but we won't get into that now."

"And how long do you expect our *arrangement* to last?"

"Six months," answered Roman.

Six months. Two grand a week for six months. More money than she knew what to do with. And all she had to do was clean his house and go to bed with him.

Exactly what Bubba wanted.

Except you didn't get paid for that, did you?

The devil of it was she could easily imagine taking Roman McCall to bed. Though Serena had suffered a lot at the hands of men, she was still a young woman with a young woman's desires. Any woman would agree that for all the man sitting next to her might have questionable intentions, he was damned fine. Oh yes. Those muscular arms and broad shoulders. His enormous hands groping her flesh.

Thick fingers sliding up into her pussy, two at once...Maybe three...

Just like the dream.

Desire flared inside her. Just once she wanted to lie down with a man who looked like a fantasy, who fucked like he gave a damn about her pleasure. Something about Roman McCall pulled at her woman's instinct; he looked like he'd give her everything she wanted with a big dick to top it off.

Sweat beaded on her neck. Yes, giving her body to this man might not be so bad... Agreeing to be a whore, then.

Nothing strange for you, said her nasty inner voice. In the past she'd traded sex for things like food and better treatment, and she wasn't proud of it. Thinking about those times made her feel sick to her stomach.

"Do you drink?" she asked.

He seemed to understand. "I'll never come to your bed drunk."

Men were always promising things. Men lied. *Say no.*

She had a choice. She imagined speaking the words. He would get in his truck and drive off and leave her here to starve with Isaiah.

Wheels turned in her head. After Mama went to jail, she lived with her Aunt Eulie. And then she died, and next came Uncle Ray, who forced her to stay home and keep house for him. And then Bubba took her down in that back room, and she made Isaiah. With no diploma she had barely landed a job at the gas station in White Florin. Then they fired her for taking too much time off when Isaiah got sick.

Two grand a week meant food for Isaiah. Clothes for Isaiah. Books. A car. Maybe even a GED. Freedom. Eventually. And no rats.

"Yes," she said. "I'll do it."

She blinked into the harsh sunlight to fight back the tears.

"Look at me," Roman said.

She looked up. He cupped her chin. "No tears, sugar," he said softly.

"Guess I'm just a little scared."

"Nothing is gonna hurt you now." She shuddered and closed her eyes. She wanted to believe him. His thumb pressed on her lower lip. His hands smelled of pine needles. "Go get your boy and get packed. We'll leave right now," he said.

She wiped her eyes. "Right now?"

"No point in waiting. Go on."

It took thirty minutes to put everything she and Isaiah owned into a suitcase. Her face burned as Roman watched her carefully fold patchwork clothes and underwear. She had fewer clothes than Isaiah and did their laundry every weekend in a tub behind the house. Luckily he'd come a day after the drying, so everything went in clean.

To the suitcase she added some of Isaiah's favorite books (there weren't many), Dinosaur, her hair combs, and some of her kitchen stuff. That was it.

"You don't have documents? Birth certificates?"

She shook her head.

"What about the boy? Where was he born?"

"In that room."

Roman rubbed his jaw. His eyes got even squintier. "You serious?"

"Yeah."

"You saw a doctor?"

"Bubba didn't want me going to the hospital. 'Cause of my age. He called some woman to see me. It worked out alright but I was sick for a while."

"What about his shots?"

"Bubba took him to the clinic. But I don't have a record of that. "

Roman looked around, taking in where Serena spent the last five years of her life. Despite her attempts to cheer the place up with little plants and flowers, nobody would ever wish to live here. The trailer was a dump. Tobacco juice stained the floorboards, and the walls were full of holes from Bubba's drunken rages.

"I hate this place," she said.

"Let's go, then."

Isaiah sat waiting in Roman's truck, wide-eyed with confusion and fear, but quiet. Roman put her suitcase in the truck bed. Instead of getting in the driver's seat right after, he took out a cigarette and smoked it. A Y-shaped vein pulsed in his forehead. He offered the box to Serena.

"I don't smoke."

His scowl deepened. "Alright."

"Are you angry?" Serena asked hesitantly. "Did I say something..."

He shook his head. "Get in the truck."

In the truck she scrambled to find Isaiah's seatbelt. Her vision blurred. It seemed too good to be true; she was waking up from the nightmare, leaving the hill, leaving those horrible men once and for all. "Ma, where are we going?" Isaiah whispered.

"To a new house. A better one," she assured him.

Isaiah's eyes widened. "My wish came true!"

"I thought it was Dinosaur's wish," she said, poking his nose.

"Are we coming back?"

"No, baby. Never."

"Did you get Dinosaur? Did you remember him?"

Hell. "He's in the suitcase, Isie. I promise I packed him."

Isaiah's lip trembled.

Serena went out to Roman. “Um. Can you get that bag down for me? I have to get something for Isaiah.”

“Can it wait?”

“Well. It’s just–never mind,” she stammered.

Roman ashed the cigarette and hauled the suitcase back out of the truck bed. Feeling foolish, she pulled out Dinosaur and handed it to Isaiah.

When she climbed up to the front seat Roman looked at her with a changed expression. She wasn’t sure what it meant.

They left the Narrows and turned up the Blue Ridge Parkway. Only a guard rail separated the Pegasus from a steep drop into a forest of white oak and pine. A curve in the road gave the illusion the asphalt suddenly ended, and Serena’s breath caught as Roman sped up towards it. Teenagers, driving home drunk in the twilight hours, had made fatal mistakes on Florin’s windy roads. But Roman knew his hills, with his foot like a stone on the gas he led them on a spinning ride up and down the very outskirts of Florin.

The blue mountains laid like fallen giants under the scorching sun. And then they vanished as the Pegasus flew into a grand hall of trees, dappled with light at the tops, the rich red clay peeking through the roots. Roman put on the radio and a John Prine song belted out. Serena twisted the end of her T-shirt around a finger and avoided looking at the stranger she had tied their lives to for the next six months.

The inside of his truck was comfortable–and immaculate. Most men Serena knew were a little tidier than pigs. Or worse than pigs. Now either Roman had bought his truck an hour ago, or he was just the type who never made a mess in his life. She couldn't even see a fingerprint on the radio dials. No cups of tobacco phlegm. No empty blue ribbon cans. No mystery burns, stains, or rips in the seats, no papers and gas station receipts crammed into cup holders. The seats smelled like wood oil. She imagined him going over the whole cab with a polishing rag every morning.

An AK-47 keyring dangled from the rearview mirror. Next to it swung an iron cross.

He likes guns and Jesus. Okay.

The "Main" McCalls lived on the opposite end of the town from Snatch Hill. To get there, Roman took a shortcut through Black Florin. They passed the black church. Women in pastel dresses and little girls in white milled about the parking lot catching up on talk before the service. Some heads turned as Roman pulled up to the stop sign. With the windows down, anybody could see Serena sitting right there in the front seat. Her fingers twitched with the urge to raise the window, but what would Roman think?

She recognized almost everybody in that parking lot. Uncle Ray had been about as far from church as a man could get, but her Great Aunt Eulie went every Sunday, rain or shine, and took Serena along. Church brought nice memories. Pretty dresses, ice cream, fried-chicken lunches, friends. But she could hear the gossip already. They would never accept her back in there. She was stained.

Ain't that Rayvaughn's niece?

What she doing in there? With him?

Well, you know that girl already. Fast.

"You go to church?" Roman asked suddenly. He hadn't said a word in twenty minutes.

"No. Isaiah ain't even baptized. I'd like to do that for him. But you know." She shrugged.

"You're an unmarried mother living in sin."

Her lips compressed. "Exactly."

"I used to park back there and listen to the music," said Roman, pointing to a spot behind the trees. "Choir's nice."

"Really? Just sit there all by yourself?"

"Yeah. Kind of strange, I guess. I don't know why I told you that. I mostly just pass right on through this side of town."

"Well, there are some nice areas in Black Florin," she said, surprised at the harsh note in his voice.

"I haven't seen 'em," said Roman.

She looked down at the golden, freckled skin on his arms. "Do you have family on that side? Maybe I know them."

Roman's sideways look made her stiffen in the seat.

"No," he said.

They turned down a private road. Serena's eyebrows traveled up her forehead as they passed endless stretches of fenced-in pasture. Up, up, up they went up the corkscrew hill.

"What's this place called?"

"This is my hill. I started living here about seven years ago. It's old family land. Took some time to clear it and lay the road."

"Oh, my goodness. That view..." She caught herself. Best not to holler like a bumpkin every time she saw some amazing sight that would be just regular to Roman.

He said, "I have four brothers. We all got some land in these hills nearby. Yonder there is my brother Rebel. He's the only one living in Florin."

"What's he like?"

"Do you honestly care?"

"I'm just asking."

Roman shifted in his seat. "Well, it's complicated with me and him is what you need to know."

Hmm.

They rumbled up to a wrought-iron gate which opened automatically, and then...

Down a road choked with wildflowers and high grass. Up another hill. Butterflies drifted past the windshield. Roman turned the radio down as they coasted to a stop next to a small green cabin with a turquoise door.

"This is where you'll stay," he said.

"Really? It's beautiful," she blurted, unable to stop herself.

She carried a drowsy Isaiah while Roman got her suitcase down. He moved the fifty-pound bag like it weighed as much as a feather. Up to the front door the trio went, Serena's heart pounding hard against Isaiah's. Roman set the bag down at the door and pointed out the number pad to Serena.

“Here’s how you change the code,” he said, and showed her. Then he turned around as she chose a new one. Ten digits.

“You gonna remember that?” he asked, turning back.

“Yes,” she said. She shifted Isaiah to her other hip, her back already aching. If the boy grew to be half the size of his daddy’s people–giants, like Roman himself–she might soon struggle to lift him.

“I’ll let you get settled tonight,” Roman said. “Then tomorrow you meet Mrs. Loving. And the rest of our arrangement will start.”

She lowered her gaze, and he caught her chin. “Serena?”

“Yeah?”

“I want you to look me in the eye when you talk to me.”

She nodded and raised her eyes to his. Was it just her imagination, or did he tense up?

He turned abruptly. “There’s food in the fridge there. Anything you need, call me on that phone. Tomorrow you’ll settle in, and we’ll talk about getting y’all some clothes and shoes.” He’d noticed Isaiah was barefoot.

“Mister Roman?” she struggled to keep eye contact.

“Yes?”

“You sure Curley can’t get in here? Don’t take this the wrong way, but your hill ain’t exactly guarded.” Isaiah stirred in her arms and she cupped his head with the back of her hand.

"There are more dangerous things on this mountain than Curley," he said.

"Like you?"

"Like me. I told you, you have nothing to worry about." He shut the door and left her to settle in.

CHAPTER 5
WILD FANTASIES

Roman's foot tapped a frustrated rhythm on the mahogany boards. All he wanted was Serena alone. But obviously, the child couldn't be left to fend for himself while his pretty mother dallied in Roman's bed.

She didn't seem like one of those women who deserted their young for a cheap thrill and a roll in the sack. Florin overflowed with females who saw no problem passing on motherhood to somebody else like a tiresome chore. Not Serena. She looked like she'd cut his throat if he messed with her boy.

Her maternal instinct reminded him of his own protectiveness over his family. If she'd showed no concern for Isaiah, Roman would find it difficult to contain his scorn for her, and that would be a problem... although in his experience, that very thing had led to the most mind-blowing sex.

Jesus. That was nothing to be proud of. Roman rubbed his jaw, hoping Serena knew what she'd signed up for. *Damaged ass.* He came to the inevitable comparison between Serena and Eileen, his first love, and Katie's mother.

Obvious differences: Eileen was a blonde, blue-eyed beauty queen. Redneck bait. One crook of her finger and he'd come a-running. Sure, he'd rope the moon to please her. Even his father liked her, which had been the first warning, in hindsight.

Eileen played him and his brothers like fiddles, then ran off to whore around with bull riders in Tulsa. Worse, she never even told him she was pregnant with his child. He had to find that out after she died, when Katie was nearly a teen. His baby spent the better part of her years under the woman's influence.

Isaiah's laugh came up from the guest house, followed by Serena's. He strained to hear more. But the laugh didn't come again.

When was the last time anybody laughed in this place?

He thought of Serena moving around down there, the child balanced on her hip. He saw in his mind's eye her face when she agreed to come with him. The girl was beautiful like Eileen, but different. Very different. As different as you could get. More earthly and real. Deep brown skin like... well, like chocolate. Them eyes. What business did a black girl have with eyes like that? They looked like amber chips. And then getting to her body... there Roman lost it completely to a lush, generous ass and large breasts, a waspish waist, the best damn pair of legs he'd ever seen... No wonder Curley didn't want to give her up.

His fantasies took a twisted turn. He imagined holding Serena down to the bed and feeding his cock inside her while she begged him for... he hardly knew what. He just wanted her to beg him. And then he wanted to give it to her. Whatever she wanted. Whatever she didn't know she wanted. He'd waited years to feel this way towards a woman, and he'd take his time savoring every bit.

For six months, the girl was his own personal fucktoy.

Sick bastard.

Don't care.

Roman turned away from the guest house, his dick losing all flexibility. He'd have her facedown in those damn pillows. Over his knee. Crying and creaming herself.

Yes. Tonight.

Serena-

Mrs. L will be there at six. Come to the house at seven. Plan to stay late.

Serena read the note again, her heart beating faster with every word. She folded the note and put it on top of the fridge out of reach from Isaiah.

"Isaiah? Your babysitter is coming today."

Isaiah still didn't understand exactly what had happened. She explained to him that Mister Roman was a nice man, a cousin of his father's, who generously gave them a place to live. Isaiah was a very understanding and trusting child, but she suspected he didn't buy the story. Maybe he sensed her own insecurities about the situation. At first he'd ran helter-skelter through the guest house rooms, screaming in happiness at all the things he'd never seen before. But a day later, with some of the excitement wearing off and his Ma just a bundle of nerves, he sat quietly, jumping at every noise. He still thought Curley would come to take them away.

That morning she saw Roman leave his house with a couple other tall men–McCalls, though not any of Bubba's people. They drove off the hill together. It would be hours before he returned, she assumed, so she set about entertaining Isaiah and inspecting their new home at the same time.

The guest house had a small study. A computer. She hadn't used one since high school. Serena sat down with Isaiah and they figured out how to use it, which took up most of the morning. Serena found paper and pencils in the desk drawer. As Isaiah drew pictures, she planned out how she would spend the forty-eight thousand dollars she'd have by the end of her six months with Roman.

1. Drivers License + car

2. GED

3. Kindergarten for Isaiah (+ friends for Isaiah)

4. Apartment

5. College (???)

She glanced down at Isaiah drawing happily on the floor. She added #7: Take a trip with Isaiah.

The day passed quickly.

A silver sedan pulled up the driveway at six o'clock on the dot. An elderly woman climbed out, bending into the backseat to take up some grocery bags.

“Is she here?” Isaiah whispered anxiously at Serena’s elbow.

“Yes. Go sit on the couch–best behavior. Okay?”

Serena met Mrs. Loving at the door.

“But what a lovely girl you are!” the old woman exclaimed, and they looked each other up and down. Mrs. Loving was a very short woman with iron gray hair. She wore a purple dress and crisp white pumps. She peered at Serena through rhinestone-framed glasses, reminding Serena all at once of her Great Aunt Eulie.

“Mind helping me with these here bags? Don’t worry, honey,” Mrs. Loving cried. “I tried to get a little of everything. There’s more in the backseat.”

Isaiah and Serena sprang to help. A bounty of food spread before their eyes, and Serena struggled not to cry on herself. She’d missed cooking real food. Mrs. Loving unloaded boxes and bottles and heaps of fruit, then lastly brought out a stack of cookbooks. “These are Roman’s. He never uses them–the man hoards books like he means to sell ‘em. I brought them from the main house.”

“Thank you,” said Serena, eyes glowing.

“I know all about the situation,” Mrs. Loving said, neatly stacking the cookbooks. “Roman explained everything. You poor lamb. Those Snatch Hill men are rotten to the bone, every one of them. How lucky you and the little man here made it out in one piece.”

Serena flushed. “You don’t mind watching Isaiah?”

"Bless it, no. Are you a good boy, honey?" she leaned down to Isaiah's level, smiling.

"Yes?" whispered Isaiah.

"Then we'll get along just fine, I reckon."

Isaiah nodded. He'd never met someone like Mrs. Loving.

"All my grandbabies are grown up now," Mrs. Loving said chattily to Serena, bustling over to the cupboards with a notepad and pen. "So I'm just up in the house with nothing to do. I know how hard it is for a young Mama like yourself to get free time. Lord, you must be desperate for it."

"I don't mind watching my son," said Serena quickly.

"But of course. I ain't saying that you don't. But Jesus knows you can't do everything alone. Sometimes you need a little help."

"So do you work for Roman?" Serena asked.

"I run his errands sometimes," Mrs. Loving answered. "The man works himself to splinters. I swear to you I've never seen him sit down longer than a minute. He was like that as a boy, too. I helped raise him, you know, after he came out of the back hills."

"The back hills?" Serena repeated. "But I thought he grew up here." The back hills were a harsh and dangerous side of Florin. People went in and never came out.

"Oh, he raised up here most of his life. But before that... Well! I reckon it ain't my business to be giving out like spare change," said Mrs. Loving, abruptly interrupting herself. "Isaiah, honey, come here and help me make a shopping list. You and me can make a pound cake while your Mama is working tonight."

Working in Roman's bed. Serena busied herself arranging the fruit.

"Okay," said Isaiah shyly.

"Do you think we need eggs?" Mrs. Loving asked him, looking over her cat-eye spectacles.

"Yes," said Isaiah, glancing at his mother. "I like eggs."

"And I'm thinking some flour, too," Mrs. Loving mused, writing it down.

"Ma makes cake with flour," said Isaiah.

"Then sugar as well, don't you think?"

"Yes. And vanilla extract."

It amused Serena that he remembered. The last time she'd made a cake for Isaiah had been his third birthday.

Mrs. Loving said, "Good thinking, honey. Why don't you add that to the list?" She handed him the pad and paper. Isaiah sat on the floor and carefully wrote out the words in his best hand.

"He can write," observed Mrs. Loving in an undertone meant only for Serena. "Very good. No school yet?"

"Not yet. I know he's a little old, maybe. But I taught him to read, and he knows some of his times tables."

The older woman patted her arm, her brown eyes gentle. "You had him young?"

Serena nodded.

Mrs. Loving looked down at Isaiah fondly. She seemed like a woman who loved children; Serena felt herself warming to her every minute. "Done with that, honey? Thank you. Ta." Isaiah handed her the list. Mrs. Loving slid it into her purse and snapped it shut. "Now, Miss Serena, I will be here during the day while you work at the big house. I'll stay until five to watch Isaiah most days. I live just on the next hill, so if you ever need me I'm a holler away. The gardener's place is over there." She pointed. "He's got his own cabin. Now, Albert likes himself a drink — or ten — on an evening, so be careful if you see him walking around. Sometimes he sleeps under the hedgerows." Her lips pinched; Serena got the feeling Mrs. Loving thought very little of Albert. "Lastly, if you and Himself run a little long conducting your business, I'd appreciate if you let me know ahead of time. I plan to be here late tonight, so don't worry. You just enjoy yourself." Serena's eyes darted to Isaiah, but of course the meaning of Mrs. Loving's words went over his head. Her face flamed; she didn't enjoy keeping the truth from Isaiah, but this was grown folks' business and he was better off not knowing.

Mrs. Loving patted her hand. "Don't worry about it, honey. Just do as Roman says and you'll be fine."

"He's very... quiet."

Before Mrs. Loving could reply, her phone buzzed. The older woman lifted her spectacles to read the text, then chuckled. "He'll be wanting to see you now. You'd better run up there, dearie. Don't keep him waiting."

Serena impulsively reached for Isaiah. "My son has never been alone without me much," she said.

"Your child is safe with me, dearie."

"If he acts up, you can't hit him. That's one thing I don't do."

"I would never dream of it," Mrs. Loving assured in such a firm voice Serena believed her. "Beating children is the surest way to raise the devil in them. I tried to tell that to Roman, when he had his daughter here. What a little hellion, that one was!" She clicked her teeth.

Serena started. "Roman has a daughter? He never said nothing about that."

"The least said about that child, the better," tutted Mrs. Loving, her cheeks turning pink. "I'll never forgive her for the way she ran off. But never mind–it ain't my business, is it? Now run along, honey. He ain't the most patient of men. You'll find that out soon enough."

A narrow alley separated the guest house from Roman's. His place was like a bigger version, painted in the same green color with an identical turquoise door. It didn't look that big from the outside, but for a man living alone it must be huge. Hopefully, as his maid, she wouldn't have to deal with the kind of male nastiness she'd endured on Pike Hill. But if the inside of his truck was any measure, then Roman must be a neat-ish kind of man.

Bracing herself, she raised the iron knocker and announced her presence against the thick oak door. Her heart slammed sideways in her chest. Her knee joints locked. If she was going to run, now would be the moment. Once Roman got her in that house there could be no escape.

But when his heavy footsteps came she remained standing in place. He opened the door, looking like he'd just showered.

He must be nearly seven feet, she thought giddily.

"Come in," he said. "Take off your shoes."

She left her battered slippers in a tray by the door. Wooden floorboards, warm under her feet.

His house smelled incredible.

"How was Mrs. Loving?" he asked in a conversational tone.

"She was nice."

"I knew you would like her."

"She said she's staying late tonight." *So you can fuck me all night long.*

"I know. Come this way."

He led her down a wide dark hall and into an open-floor, cozy room. Serena's eyes popped open. This place was... gorgeous. Antique sofas upholstered in crushed emerald velvet, oil paintings hanging off paneled walls that ended some two dozen feet in the air, meeting exposed pine rafters. Her bare feet were introduced to a plush carpet, and Roman explained how to draw back the complicated system of drapes to expose sunlight from French windows. He called them French windows but to Serena they just looked like big, expensive slabs of glass that would let in freezing temperatures right along with the sunlight.

Next he swept her into an unfamiliar room with a wide mahogany table that could comfortably seat a family of twelve. “That’s the dining room,” he said briefly.

“Lovely settings,” she commented.

“I didn’t pick ‘em out.”

“Who did?”

“Eileen. They were her mother’s. She left ‘em with me.”

“Who is Eileen? Your wife?”

“No,” he said, a little sharply. “I ain’t married.”

“Guess I should have asked that before I came here.”

“Too late now,” he said.

Then, into the kitchen. Roman showed her the antique gas stove, the pantry, the fridge. Serena nodded along, barely hearing a word. She was busy wondering what kind of cleaning he expected from her. The house was spotless. Just like his truck. Not a speck of dust anywhere.

He opened the spice cupboard. Serena noticed all the little bottles arranged in alphabetical order. “If you need anything in here, let me know,” he said. “You can add it to the list on the fridge.”

She squinted at the list. His handwriting was terrible.

“Alright,” she said, watching him tweak the position of one spice bottle so it stacked neatly in the row with the others.

Obsessive. Likes control.

“This way now,” he said, shutting the cabinet. “You don’t have questions?”

"Oh no," she lied. "Everything sounds good to me."

In all her days she'd never seen a house so fine, like she'd stepped into the pages of a Home & Country catalog. And this man lived here by himself? Where was the daughter?

"Mrs. Loving..." Serena began awkwardly.

He turned and looked down his nose at her. "Pardon?"

"Your, um, daughter," Serena said, forcing herself not to shrink back.

"Oh," he said. "She's gone. Her room is that white door in that hallway." He paused, then said roughly, "I don't want you going in there. Ever."

"Got it," said Serena.

"Come on this way."

They passed the forbidden door, and Roman led her down a long hallway towards another one. "This is my office. If I catch you snooping in here, you're gone. Understand? If you need me, just knock and I'll come out."

"Yes, I understand."

They doubled back through the hall. Two flights of stairs book ended this side of the house, leading to one end of the large hallway which itself branched into smaller rooms. On this end, the hallway stopped at a carved door made from some heavy type of wood. Roman took an iron key out of his pocket and unlocked it. He held the door for her.

She knew it was his bedroom even before he clicked the light on. His smell, clean and mouthwatering, overwhelmed her senses. She hovered in the doorway. His touch at the small of her back made her jump. "Don't be scared," he said.

"I'm not."

"You're shaking." He clicked on the light. A soft, sexy bedroom light.

Red mahogany furniture, a four-poster, a landscape painting above the bed of a six-pointer, poised in a shady glade as if it had just noticed the hunter behind it. The bed looked comfortable and wide.

"You must like the color green," she said in a wobbling voice.

"I do."

He steered her towards the four-poster. She saw something red and silky laid out on the emerald sheets.

"W-what's that?"

His voice matched her whisper. "I want you to try it on."

"Oh."

Just like that he moved from terrifying to sexy.

"Bathroom's over there. Unless you want to strip for me here."

"Um, one second." He handed her the garment, and she fled into the bathroom.

He'd caught her nodding. The sneaky bastard.

When the door clicked shut behind her she quivered like a beech in a gale. *Calm down. He ain't even touched you yet.* Serena leaned over the marble counter and took deep gulping breaths. Her reflection looked bug-eyed and sick. *It's for Isaiah. You and Isaiah, going on vacation together. Isaiah going to a private school. Getting your license. Your own place. No Bubba, no Curley, no goddamned McCalls ever again.*

Amazement eclipsed her nerves as the bathroom came into focus. Opulent as the rest of the house, with marble walls, marble countertops, and a tub like something from a playboy mansion. Firstly, it was effing huge. Definitely meant for a man Roman's size, and maybe a female companion. Second, it had an electric pad with all these buttons. Instead of writing, each button had a symbol on it. Maybe he'd want to take a bath with her... Why did she like the idea?

Quiet as a mouse, Serena opened his cabinet. Toothbrush, floss, and Magnums. A Roman-sized box of magnums to match the Roman-sized everything else. Her throat went dry.

She heard him moving in the bedroom. Remembering Mrs. Loving's warning about her impatient employer, Serena shut the cabinet and summoned her nerve. She pulled off her T-shirt and cutoffs, cringing at how dusty they looked against the finery that surrounded her. She hooked her thumbs into the band of her panties. Her big, cotton, bought-in-an-eight-pack-at-Walmart-three-years-ago panties. She scrolled them down, kicking them under the pile.

She picked up the red silk teddy.

The fabric moved through her fingers like water. She slid it on, gasping at the slightly cold material against her skin.

She turned back to the mirror.

The red color came out vivid against her dark skin and made her hazel eyes look yellow. Her large breasts pushed against the fabric, nipples perking up in the cold bathroom. It looked whorish. She turned this way and that. Years of dressing down her slim-thick figure caused her to barely recognize herself.

On an impulse, she took the scrunchie and pins from her hair. The thick knotty puffs lifted over her shoulders and floated around her head. She shook them out. Serena never wore her hair down, and her hands-off (lazy) approach meant it had grown thick and long. She needed two hands to contain the mass of it.

She'd worn nothing like the red teddy in her life. It whispered against her bare skin, sliding into places that were hot and forbidden.

He'll like this. I want him to like it.

She thought of the box of magnums and a jolt of desperate female longing went all the way to her bare toes.

When she emerged, Roman was sitting on the bed. She stepped slowly into the light, towards him, heart thudding in her throat.

Serena slid out of the bathroom, looking like a doe trapped in a hunter's sights. She tugged at the straps of the teddy. "It fits," she whispered.

An understatement. Roman felt the bottom fall out of his chest. He rasped, "Come here."

She floated towards him. His hands came up and ghosted the curve of her hips. "My God," he said. "My God."

Her lips parted. They studied each other; Roman for once not caring that a woman had left him weak and unguarded. She was the most beautiful creature he'd ever laid eyes on.

The midnight color of her skin went on for miles without a single mark or flaw, except for the deep bruises on her arms. She had a birthmark on her thigh shaped like the print of a man's thumb. He pressed his own into it, feeling her softness yielding under him.

And she smelled like a pot of sugar put on a low fire. Reaching around to cup the backs of her thighs, he opened his knees and guided her to stand between them. Her arms came up hesitantly and rested on his shoulders.

"I like this," he said, struggling for words. "You like it?"

"Yes," she whispered simply.

He skimmed her skin. So soft, so smooth. Dark as teak. He pressed his face into her silk-clad stomach.

Here, her smell enveloped him. Women were truly the most beautiful things God ever made. The silk slid against his lips. He caught some with his teeth, eyes screwed shut. Breathe. His chest cramped under the pressure of his lust. He'd denied himself this for years. So many long and bitter nights. And now he had a female here, his very own, to comfort him and give him the thing he needed.

"You'll need more clothes," he said. "More. Like this."

"Okay."

He forced himself to pull away. “Go to that dresser. Take the magazine on there, and the pen.”

“Okay...”

He watched her cross the room and lift the magazine off the dresser. Her eyes widened. “This is for sex toys.”

“Don’t worry about that.” *For now.* “Go to the back. To the garments.”

She sat on the bed next to him, worrying her lower lip between her teeth. “Oh, my goodness.”

“Pick what you want.”

“They’re so expensive.”

“I’ll enjoy taking ‘em off you.”

He watched her flip gingerly through the catalog. She circled all of his favorites, though he kept his expression neutral so as not to influence her choice too much. When she finished, she replaced the magazine exactly where she found it.

“Thank you,” she said politely.

“You need new clothes besides that. Regular clothes. We’ll deal with that tomorrow. And your boy as well. I noticed he’s growing out of what he has.”

“I can buy him clothes myself, from what you pay me.”

“The boy is kin to me too. I can’t have him running around in rags.”

She stiffened. “Isaiah don’t wear rags. Sure, he’s growing, but I would never–”

"Calm down. I wasn't taking a dig at your motherhood."

"You said I dress him in rags."

"I didn't mean it like that." He pulled her close and kissed her neck. She instantly went soft in his arms.

"Take it easy, darling. You'll need that fire for when I really piss you off."

"You planning to piss me off? It won't end well for you."

He huffed a laugh. "It'll happen, eventually."

She leaned back in his arms, fingers curling against his scalp. "You one of those men that blows up on a dime, or do you just sit and stew on it?"

"The first."

"I really don't want to see you angry." She looked down at his hands, which nearly spanned her entire waist.

"I won't ever lay lands on you. Nor Isaiah. That ain't what I brought you here for." He stroked her thighs with both thumbs. "You believe me?"

"Yes. But..." She drew a shaky breath. "You've been very generous to me. In my experience no man is generous for free. Sooner or later he starts makin' impossible demands."

"You an expert on men?"

"Just certain kinds."

"I'm going to make one demand right now, Serena."

"W-what's that?"

He rolled the straps of the teddy down, baring her breasts for the first time. Breathing hard, Roman palmed her soft feminine flesh. Brown flesh. Brown skin. The contrast against his paler hands shorted out his brain.

Her nipples were the color of strong coffee and the size of cherries. They capped heavy tits that splayed out across her chest, tapering at the ends like torpedoes, a perverse shape that spun visions of him lying back while she straddled him and fed them into his mouth.

She held up the teddy at her stomach, blocking his view from the rest of her. That wouldn't do. He took her hand away and dragged it down, over the smooth stomach, the generous hips... her pussy.

He looked up. Her lips were parted, her eyes bright with fear and desire both. Roman kissed her belly as he parted her lips with his thumb.

"Oh," she whimpered. He found the gooey center of her arousal and spread it over her entrance slowly, slowly, though every male instinct demanded he just fuck her. He wanted her to enjoy a man's touch.

His thumb entered her slowly. *Hot. Wet. Mine.*

"Serena."

"Y-yes?"

"When was the last time you took a man in you?"

"Three years."

Her inner feminine softness tightened on his thumb. "Not since Curley. Everybody — too scared — "

"Right. Your curse. I heard about that." His other hand kneaded her thick ass. "Sounded like bullshit to me."

"I ain't cursed."

"No, darling." He laughed softly. "Far from it, I think." He slowly fucked his thumb into her pussy. Her inner walls caressed and squeezed his digit. Virgin-tight.

"Should I lie down?" she gasped.

"Hot for it already?"

"Isn't that what you want?"

"Best we don't rush it." He took his finger out and reached for his belt. "Bend over the bed."

"You want me to take this off?"

The girl was a natural submissive. Fucking Christ. "No," he said.

She rolled the teddy back up and bent over the bed obediently, standing on tiptoe with her ass in the air like she wanted him to fuck it. The teddy rode up between her cheeks, her bare pussy peeking out.

He unbuckled his belt. His dick ached, so hard for her. A bead of pre-ejaculate swelled at the end. Roman fisted his cock in a crushing grip, quelling the urge to bury it inside her. She was wet, but still unprepared. It would hurt her. Why did the idea get him off?

He wiped his mouth with his wrist. *Calm down.* Sometimes he got too aggressive in bed; but he had to be so careful. The girl had been hurt before, used and abused. She wouldn't appreciate too rough a handling.

Serena turned around and saw him stroking his dick over her ass.

"Oh my God."

"What?"

"It's bigger than I thought," she whispered, her eyes glowing with sudden hunger.

She's perfect.

"Lay down the other way. On your back," he said.

She rolled over. He leaned forward, slid and arm under her waist and hauled her up the bed. She bounced, and her arms naturally came up around his neck.

And then they were kissing.

All his ideas of careful seduction drained from his brain. She kissed him like they were old lovers, and while half of Roman rebelled against this sweetness, distrusting it, the other half found itself torn, and then dragged, deeper into the embrace.

She sucked and bit at his lips, as if trying to get something from him, and he gave it to her in deep, passionate kisses with his tongue in her mouth and his hands cupping and squeezing her ass. Her whole body responded to his touch; she curved up against him, her hands digging into his curly black hair. He could smell her arousal and it drove him wild. Still kissing her, and kissing her, he plunged his fingers back into her cunt and began fucking her down to his first knuckle. She cried out *yesyesyesyes.* He pulled away from her lips and bit her throat like an animal claiming dominance, and Serena exploded, her pleasure splattering on his sheets, on his fist, his naked dick.

Woah.

He'd never been with a woman who could do that. Roman pulled away, all the blood in his body flooding his cock. He opened his mouth and no human sound came out. She squirmed against the last throes of her orgasm, her eyes slitted and full of tears. She reached out and grabbed his dick and stroked it right against her velvet-soft stomach. He looked impossibly huge lined up against her like that.

"You want to do it now?" she whispered. She stroked him, cupped his heavy balls. "It's so big."

"Yeah," he gritted.

"I can get you off like this," she said. He blinked, and suddenly her incredible tits were wrapped around his aching length like pillows.

"Jesus God. You little... so beautiful... whore." He leaned his weight on his arms, panting hard. "Where... how..."

Did Bubba make her do that? Did Curley?

He slid his cock through the pillowy channel of her breasts, bumping hard against her chin. "Oh God. Just like that..." And then she took his dick in her mouth.

Serena tried to push down the rising panic in her chest, forcing herself to be a receptacle for his lust — a willing whore. Adrenaline pumped through her as Roman's massive frame trapped hers in the bed.

Flashbacks. Moments of pain and humiliation burst out of the locked vault in her mind, but she focused on the clean male scent of the man above her, of his beautiful body and the way his handsome face grew tight with need as he touched her. He had a big, pretty dick too...he forced it deeper.

She forced her mind blank. Reconstructing her thoughts with each sensation Roman's beautiful male body gave her. She wanted him. He was just like the men in her dreams. She cupped his balls and stroked his big dick, her head swimming with pleasure. Her mouth made a heaven for him to slide into, and every gasp and moan he made thrilled her to the core. She was in control now; he wanted her... He inched a little more down her throat.

CAN'T BREATHE.

She pulled away from him, gasping, leaving a sticky trail between his cock and her swollen lips. One hand went to her throat as if to pull away an invisible chokehold. She blinked hard, forgetting where she was.

"Serena?" Roman said. "Hey. Woah."

"I'm fine," she mumbled.

He cupped her chin and thumbed a bead of shiny spit from her lips. "Too fast?"

She gulped. "I don't know."

"We'll stop, honey," he said quietly.

"Okay." She sat up, embarrassed, and began sliding the teddy on. Roman shook his head and pulled her down to the bed. "Just lay here a second," he said. Then he looked embarrassed. "If you want."

She lay down next to him. He took her in his arms and pillowed her head on his chest. He stroked her back. The silence between them became hypnotic and strange. Roman smelled *so good.*

He tightened his hold until she nestled closer into the steady heat of his body. He held her just like she held Isaiah — protectively.

Don't go getting these ideas. It's not like that for him and you know it.

But she fell asleep and so did he. Some hours later a call from Mrs. Loving woke them up from the extended nap. Roman rolled over and read the time off his cellphone. "Shit."

"My God. We fell right asleep."

"Mm." He cupped her ass and tucked her closer against him, answering the phone with his other hand. Mrs. Loving informed him that Isaiah was in bed, and her episode of *Preacher Man* had ended, and would they finish their business soon?

"She'll be down in a minute," Roman replied. He hung up and sighed.

"You going to sleep now?" Serena murmured.

"Naw," he said, sitting up and reaching for his belt. "Got to head back out. I got business in town."

"Mister Roman?"

"Yeah?"

She rested her chin on her hand. "What is it you do, exactly, for the McCalls?"

"I am the McCalls. I outright own most of the land— the other clans rent from me at a huge discount."

"And in Black Florin? You own that too?"

"About two-thirds of it," he said. Serena's eyebrows went up, but Roman went on smoothly, "Basically my job is to manage our property, run the feed store and keep the wheels greased on any other business venture."

She knew what he meant. "You grow dope with the Snatch Hills, don't you? And the Green Trees?"

"Yeah, that too." He snapped on the belt. "The less you know about that the better." He gave her a long look, traveling up her bare legs to the teddy bunched around her pussy. His eyes burned. "Now I think you best get gone, sweetheart," he said quietly. "Or I might just be tempted for round two."

Serena quickly dressed. Between her legs felt sticky and wet. When she emerged from the bathroom Roman was sitting on the edge of the bed, pulling on his enormous boots. She saw the Glock resting on the nightstand and froze, for a wild moment thinking it was meant for her.

"You gonna shoot somebody?"

"It's for protection," he said. Adding, when he saw her deer-in-headlights look, "It's not loaded. Now time to go, Serena."

She slipped out of the room, chest tight. *He's right. I better just leave it alone.* There would be time to make up for her awkward freeze-up in bed. Time enough to show him she could do her job. She hoped. The last thing she wanted was Roman to change his mind about keeping her here.

Six months, she reminded herself. *Six months, and you won't be nobody's whore ever again.*

CHAPTER 6
THE BATH

Roman left McCall's Supply and Feed near midnight. The parking lot was dark, and so he didn't see the man until he'd stepped up to the driver's side of his truck. Something moved in the window's reflection. His neck prickled. Roman ducked just in time to escape the deadly blow.

The crowbar shattered the truck window, missing the intended target of Roman's skull. Roman spun around the next attack, grabbing the man by the scruff and wrenching the arm holding the crowbar down and backwards. The man's howl echoed in the empty parking lot. Roman shoved a knee into his spine, crunching the man into the pavement while he checked for another weapon. No gun, just a knife. The man must be a fool. Roman snapped his own gun from his waistband. He jammed the weapon into the base of the man's skull, his finger ghosting the trigger.

"Move," he said.

Roman had been the last person to leave the warehouse. They stood in an empty parking lot out of range of the cameras. Good. It would have been tiresome to have to wipe the footage later. As they moved into the trees, they became invisible.

He thrust the man down into the leaves. "Who are you?"

"Fuck you," the man panted.

From the stink, the bastard came from the back hills. Roman backed away and racked the slide on his Glock. "Turn around. Slowly."

The man did so, his hands on his head.

Roman looked him up and down. No; he'd never seen the fella before.

"What's your name?"

"Terry."

"Who sent you? Curley?"

"Rain McCall sent me."

"Is that right?" said Roman coldly.

"That's right. Your little brother's owin' me money, and I come to collect."

Rain. Roman seethed. He was going to kill the little junkie with his bare hands.

"How much does he owe you?"

"Six grand," huffed Terry. "Plus interest."

Roman almost laughed. “You think I’m walking around with six grand hangin’ out my ass?”

“You’re the main McCall,” said Terry. “You got money fallin’ from the sky. I was gonna bust you up and make you open the safe in that place.”

“I wouldn’t be any good to you with my brains stuck to a crowbar. That’s what guns are for.”

Terry scowled. “The wife was bitchin’ and I forgot my piece.”

“That was a mistake.”

“Tell me about it,” grumbled Terry. He raised his chin. “You gonna shoot me?”

“In just a minute.” Roman dug in his pocket for a cigarette and flicked one out of the box. Terry picked it off the ground. “Thank ye.”

Roman lit it for him, keeping his gun trained on the man’s head. Then he lit one for himself, one-handed. They smoked quietly.

“How long’s my brother been buying drugs off you?” Roman inquired.

“Couple months. He likes them blue pills. Make you feel all warm and fuzzy.”

“What’s he done with your six grand?”

“Don’t know, but he stole it and I got proof.”

“You afraid to die?”

Terry exhaled smoke. “There’s worse things.”

"You love your wife?"

"Nope."

"Any children?"

"They's grown."

Terry finished the cigarette and flicked the smoking butt into the leaves. "Get it over with, McCall."

"Don't rush me, Terry."

"You're one scary motherfucker. They all said that, but I didn't believe it." Terry sighed. "I reckon you can shoot me now. Better just get it done."

"You in a hurry?"

"Everybody's got to die sometime. I owed people that money, and they gonna kill me worse if I don't give it back. Hope the little shithead spent it good. Your brother."

"Next time bring a gun," said Roman.

"I'll remember that."

"Who you owe that money to?"

Terry shook his head. "Snatch hills. More McCalls. I'm right sick of your fuckin family, you know that?"

"That makes two of us," said Roman.

As the man laughed quietly, Roman shot him.

Roman called up Sam Bailey and waited twenty minutes in the parking lot for his cousin to arrive. They moved the body into the bed of Roman's truck and covered it with bags of feed. Not as if Roman expected to get stopped and searched. The law worked differently for McCalls in Florin.

As Sam approached, Roman fished through the dead man's pockets and found his keys. The cousins did a walkabout and found the beat-up Chevy parked a ways down the hill. Sam climbed in and drove the truck to a distant place while Roman followed in his truck. Sam parked the truck in a ditch, left the keys in the ignition and got into Roman's passenger seat. In this part of Florin, it would be weeks or months before someone happened on the vehicle. Roman had a suspicion no one would come looking for Terry soon — at least not in the open.

An hour later the cousins entered the old back hills mine. Ninety years ago an explosion widowed a hundred women and closed the mine down permanently. The desolate place was surely haunted; full of echoes and ghosts. Any trees that survived the poison soil bent like overgrown fingernails towards the earth.

He and Sam hauled Terry's body out of the truck bed and rolled it onto a tarp, then dragged the dead man up through the scree and dust to the mouth of an abandoned shaft. Sam kicked Terry in, jumping back as if the man would come to life and grab his ankles on the way down. The corpse seemed to fall forever before it thudded against the bottomless bottom. Both men stared into the black hole for a few minutes.

"Who was that?" asked Sam finally.

"Terry."

"Who's Terry?"

"Back hills fella. He seemed alright."

"Poor bastard."

"Yeah."

Sam eyed Roman. "Thirsty?"

"You read my mind," said Roman.

He changed clothes at Sam's place, and the cousins went to one of the honky-tonks in the foothills. Baileys and Green Trees and even Snatch Hills fluttered in and out. There was dancing and whores, and though Roman had himself plenty of the first, he avoided the second. He asked if anybody had seen Rain lately. No one had.

Liquor dribbled on his clothes, men made business offers in his ears, and women gave him squeezes in interesting places that didn't have the usual effect. His mind wandered even as his cousins caroused and partied around him, fighting and fucking and stomping to the tune of an Appalachian fiddle as the night elapsed into dawn.

When light touched the hills Roman took his leave, still too drunk to drive. Used to be he'd take those roads no matter how sauced he was, but ever since Katie came to live with him he'd tried to set a good example. Folks died on these roads all the time coming back from parties too wasted. Following the habit he chose–perhaps foolishly–to walk home. The act sobered him up some. As miles passed under his boots, he drove away the vision of the mineshaft, of Terry, with thoughts of his warm bed... And a warm sweet woman he could tumble in it.

Headlights scored the darkness. Roman turned, his heart racing. Maybe this was it–the end. Payment for his sins.

Shot down on a mountain road, no witnesses. The old busted van pulled up beside him.

Ben Simpson rolled down the window, looking Roman over.

"Need a ride?" the black man said.

Roman reached for his gun.

Ben held up two hands. "Don't get froggy, McCall. It ain't like that."

"I ain't goin' your way."

"You don't know where I'm goin'," Ben replied.

Roman considered. His halfway-sober brain urged him on. A hard number of miles lay between himself and his house, and besides, he was curious. He climbed up.

The owner of Ben's Hot Chicken said, "I figured we ought to talk."

"About what?"

"I heard from my nephew. He's coming back home."

"With my daughter, I hope, or he'd best not come back at all."

Ben's voice hardened. "According to my nephew, your daughter left him at a road stop outside Oklahoma City. She drove off with his car–my car–and left him there like an unwanted dog."

Roman couldn't say that didn't sound like his Katie. He grunted, "I haven't heard from her in weeks. I send her money, that's all she wants from me."

"You sent somebody to find her?" Ben Simpson asked.

"She's stayin' with her grandmother."

"Junior says the old woman had dementia, and your girl was stealin' her pension. She ran off with the bullriders, Junior said. I don't know what happened to that granny, nor do I care, but your daughter ain't even in Tulsa no more, McCall."

"Jesus wept," Roman muttered, rubbing his eyes.

"I'm bringing my nephew home. I'm asking you not to move against him. He's a good boy, even though he ain't got no sense."

"If he was so good, he would have left my girl alone."

Ben eyed him sideways. "Once, your brother Rebel said to me, 'people ain't checkers'. They don't just stay where you lay 'em down. They move around. Mix it up. Maybe that's alright." His knobby hands gripped the wheel. "What do you think? I guess I can tell already."

"I think Rebel's an idealist."

"Some would say a fool."

"Some would." But it was something he admired about Rebel: his little brother's optimism carried him far. Rebel was happy now, even with Katie bullshit weighing on him the way it weighed on Roman. Rebel had found a woman and a purpose. Roman couldn't say the same.

Ben Simpson sighed. "I know you ain't a friend to black people, McCall. But I'm hoping both sides of this place can come together over what matters–raising families and working hard–since the biggest obstacle to that is now dead."

"Everything's got an order and a place," Roman replied, hearing his father's words coming from his own mouth.

"And our place is on the bottom, is what you're saying."

"If you don't like it, you can always leave."

Ben shook his head. "We won't have to. Look at your daughter, your brother. Everything's changing in this day and age. Give it a while, won't be a Florin man walking around *without* some mixed blood in him. Of course, some can hide it better than others."

The underhanded jab didn't escape Roman. It was nearly funny. All his life he could pass for white, and people might speculate just what kind of creature he was, but never pinned him down. They just called him "gypsy". Now these days it seemed like the truth was written on his forehead... maybe literally. Roman passed a hand over his growing curls. He'd shorn his hair all his life, but after Duke's murder he let it grow wild and untamed. Let them stare. Let them talk.

His physical differences from the other McCalls put a target on his back early in life. It taught him that being a McCall wasn't just about blood. It was about strength, hard work, and cunning. Men who sneered at his dubious breeding were merely compensating for some inner weakness. And if they were fool enough to challenge him, they quickly regretted it. Roman fought for his right to the McCall name, and he was proud of that.

But sometimes, being a McCall didn't seem like such a good thing.

Most of the fighting Roman did in his younger days happened in his own house. Roman's father Duke was a thoroughbred McCall; his parents had been second cousins. In private Duke threw Roman's mixed blood at him like a weapon.

Halfbreed. Son of a whore. McCalls are strong. McCalls are tough. You want to be a McCall, nigger boy, you get tough like me.

So Roman did.

He recalled the moment vividly. He'd been nineteen. He and Duke were arguing–fuck if he remembered why–and Duke charged him. Roman knocked the old man clean onto his ass. Rang him like a goddamned bell. Duke came at him again. Roman put the wall at his back just like he'd been taught, and grabbed his father's fist before it could shatter his jaw. Roman's strength surprised them both. Their eyes met, and in that electric moment Roman saw real fear in his father's eyes. Like a wretch who raises a wolf from a cub and wakes to find it full grown and lunging for his throat. And Roman let the bastard have it. He fought with nineteen years of bitter rage and put Duke in the hospital.

After that, Duke never tried it with him again. There even blossomed between father and son a kind of respect. Roman became the silent operator of the McCall family and his father's right hand. There were even good times among the bad. But one thing would always stand between them, unable to be reconciled, and that thing was what Duke had done to Roman's mother.

Roman had been torn from some vital part of his being and shaped crudely into Duke's weapon. Implanted with the man's beliefs. Roman learned to hate the other half of himself and sought to sew up the hole inside him by committing everything that remained to the McCalls. And for years he nursed a somewhat childish bitterness towards his mother's people. After all, none of them came to save her from Duke. They didn't save him.

Roman craved acceptance like any man. He got none from the McCalls, and none from the other silent half of Florin. But maybe men like him could never be accepted. Maybe they shouldn't be. Maybe they were just broken.

He stared out for a long time into the darkness, over the mountain which he now ruled. Ben Simpson allowed the silence.

"I won't make laws between our sides the way Duke did," Roman said to the old man. "I'll let your nephew return. But the McCalls will rule this mountain as long as this mountain stands. Know that."

"A house divided cannot stand," said Ben. "And neither can this mountain."

As he opened the front door to his house, the smell of frying bacon awakened all his senses. Serena's sweet voice called out from the kitchen. Roman had not expected that; he'd half forgotten about his new hired help. *Hired whore.* She bent over his dining table, laying down a plate of greasy, delicious fare. Bacon and biscuits, gravy, grits, orange slices and grapes, plus a pot of steaming coffee.

"Mrs. Loving came early. Figured I'd make you breakfast," she said, smiling at him.

Roman wondered if he'd stepped into some waking dream. The girl's eyes shone with friendly warmth and he felt uncharacteristically shy.

"You made biscuits, too?" he grunted.

"I started them at my house and brought them over."

He lowered his weary self into a chair. "Thank you," he said gratefully.

"I'm just glad to have a working kitchen again," Serena said. "Do you want orange juice?"

"I'll take the coffee first."

"Alright."

She poured it for him without spilling a drop. Every move Serena made was graceful and feminine. "Cream or sugar?" she asked, laying out the dishes.

"Neither."

"Ugh." She returned the creamer to the fridge, then came right back out and sat next to him. Now she played with the edge of the napkin. She was so funny. Bold as a bee one moment, shy the next.

He pushed a plate of toast at her. She smiled and started slathering a wedge of sourdough with jam. "I ate already, you know."

"So?" he grunted.

She waved the toast at him. "Don't try to fatten me up. I got enough to lose."

"Bullshit."

Most people didn't take breakfast with the hired help. *But I don't think of her that way.*

"Did you have a good night?" he asked.

"I slept good," she replied, looking him up and down. "What about you?"

He thought about Terry sliding into the mineshaft.

"It was fine," he said.

"Where did you go?" She sniffed his shirt. "You smell like whiskey and cigarettes."

It gave him an idea. After he finished the massive meal, he took Serena's hand and led her to the bedroom.

"But–the dishes–"

"Leave 'em."

He rinsed off the worst of the night's grime before he filled the tub and called her in.

She sat on the edge of the marble and leaned over him. "You want me to get in there with you?"

"When was the last time you had one?"

"I showered this morning," she said defensively. "I know I don't stink."

"I mean a bath like this."

She blinked. "Well...never. Maybe when I was a baby or something."

"Get in."

"Really? You serious?"

He flicked water at her. She eagerly shed her clothes. Roman had kept the lights dim, and the narrow window showed the warm sunshine of the very early morning. It made a pleasing effect on her dark skin. Serena stepped into the steaming water, naked.

"Oh! It's hot! Roman, I'll melt."

He squinted at her through the haze of steam. "Come here." She slowly drifted towards him, and turned around so her back tucked against his chest. Her bun poked his chin. "You got more hair than I don't know what," he murmured.

"You can take it down if you want," she said, as if sensing his curiosity.

She leaned forward, and Roman slowly removed the pins and the tie from the heavy mass of it. "Now you're truly naked," he murmured. She shivered.

He spread her kinky tresses out, combing his fingers through the ends until it hung down, more or less, over her shoulders.

The heat of the water drugged them both. Roman leaned back against the marble, circling Serena's stomach with both arms.

"Did you see another woman last night?" she asked softly.

"No." He rested his chin on her shoulder.

"Did you shoot somebody?" She said it as a joke, but Roman went still and she jerked her head up, eyes widening.

"I did," he confessed.

"My God."

"I don't want to talk about it," he added.

"Good, 'cause I wasn't gonna ask."

She searched his face, then turned back around, wiggling closer to him. *She really ain't afraid of me. Go figure.* Serena snuggled right up, resting a hand on his thigh under the water. "Did he deserve it?" she said.

"I thought you weren't gonna ask."

She ran her hand up his leg. Roman stroked her soft stomach and said, "He tried to kill me, so I killed him. It ain't for me to say what he deserved."

"You killed a lot of men before?"

"A few."

Everybody's got to die sometime.

"Hmm," she said. She grew soft and almost boneless in his arms, truly melting into the hot mint-scented water.

"Does it scare you?" he forced himself to ask.

"What? You killing somebody?"

"Yeah."

"I don't know. I guess I just trust you had a reason." She spoke slowly. "You don't seem like you enjoyed it. Curley and Bubba liked hurting things. They never lost a wink of sleep over nothing that they did. You're not like that, I think. You walked in here looking like you was carrying the weight of the world. Maybe I'm a fool, but I trust you."

He separated the incredible kinks and coils of her hair gently with his fingers. Serena sighed and tilted her head back. The water stretched it out, and Roman started from the ends and worked his way up, pulling apart the tangles.

"You want to go to bed?" she whispered as her nipples stiffened in the water.

"I'd pass out on top of you."

She shuddered. "I wouldn't even care."

She reached around and cupped his hard dick under the water. Steam bloomed between them. Almost sleepily she stroked his aching cock, her head lolling against his neck. It felt so good. Too good. Roman grabbed her wrist and stopped her.

"Why?" she whispered, looking up at him with her pretty toffee-colored eyes.

"I'll take care of it."

"You sure?"

"Just sit here a while. We don't have to do nothing."

"But you're so hard."

"Yeah. Just...ah. Shit. Shit."

Her hand walked up the back of his neck and threaded through his growing curls. Her other hand stroked him. *Squeeze. Stroke. Squeeze. Stroke.* His legs bucked under the water. He groped her large breasts, pinching her nipples until they stood out fully erect.

"Let me put it in your mouth."

He sat on the wide edge of the tub and she knelt between his knees. Her whiskey eyes looked up at him in a sexual delirium. She sucked on him, using her hands and tongue. Slow, languid strokes. He emptied himself into her, and she swallowed it.

"You're so beautiful."

"Thank you," she whispered.

He toweled her dry and carried her into the bed. They lay there naked and tangled together. Serena hummed as her eyes drifted shut.

"Where's that from?" He grunted.

"Huh? Oh, it's an old song."

He passed her his phone. "Find it for me."

"Okay," she said, a little surprised.

"Uh huh." She scrolled down through his phone and stifled a laugh. Her shy voice teased, "Mister Roman. What the hell do you be listening to?"

Roman snatched the device from her so fast she started giggling for real. He connected it to the bluetooth. Serena looked startled.

"You have speakers in here?"

"Yeah, country girl, I do."

"Shut up."

They laid back in the bed and listened to the sweet slow protest of Nina Simone.

"Nobody ever did it better," Serena sighed. She reached down and took his hand. Rested it on her chest.

Before he knew it, Roman was dead asleep.

CHAPTER 7
THE YOUNGEST

"Who is that girl in your kitchen?" demanded Ross McCall, throwing his briefcase into the leather chair. Already Roman's youngest brother looked as if the mountain air was making his stomach hurt. Ross lived in Rowanville and avoided Florin like a plague-hole.

"Her name is Serena."

"Your maid?"

"That's right."

"She's making a lemon meringue pie," Ross said, raising both eyebrows.

Good–it was his favorite.

"You fucking her?" said Ross bluntly. "She looks way too young for you."

The youngest McCall brother paced around the study, picking up things and putting them down. He stopped dead in his tracks as Roman let the silence stretch.

"You're addled," Ross said, horrified. "You're sleeping with that girl. A Black girl. Hell, she looks about Katie's age!"

"She's older than that," said Roman quickly.

"By what? A fortnight? If this is some kind of nervous breakdown–"

"It's not."

Ross loved the sound of his own voice. The boy could start an argument in an empty room.

"You can lecture me later. Just tell me what you found so you can scuttle off back to your fundraising luncheon or whatever the hell," Roman told him.

Ross seated himself and got down to business with a sarcastic tilt to his aristocratic mouth. "Alright. You want the long or the short version?"

"The extremely short version, unless my life is in some kind of imminent danger."

"You aren't worried about the possibility that our father's murderer might target you next?"

"Not really," Roman confessed.

Ross's eyes narrowed. "How interesting. May I ask why?"

"I think a woman killed him. And knowing Pa, it's likely she had a damned good reason, and I got nothing to worry about."

"Very interesting."

"It's just a hunch, and I can't even explain it." Roman shrugged. "But speak your piece, Ross. I won't hold you up."

The younger man leaned back in his chair like a college professor about to stump an impertinent student. "Well, Roman, to put it plainly, I'm inclined to think it was someone from the other side of Florin who killed our father," he said.

"*Black Florin*?"

"Yep," said Ross.

"Explain."

"Rebel."

"Explain in complete sentences," Roman gritted.

Ross's mouth made a line. "Well, our dear brother said he didn't want me stirring up trouble over on that side of town, even when I pointed out that Pa was killed right on the border. In fact, when I talked to Rebel, he doth protested too much if you catch my drift. Almost like he knew something."

Now that was interesting. Rebel had many connections to the Black Florin grapevine. It was fully possible he knew some vital information to the case, but wasn't telling.

Ross continued, "At the very least, the fact that it never occurred to any of us to suspect the folks with the biggest motive for killing Pa is concerning. You know he ran roughshod over those people for years."

Yes, Roman knew. He nodded. "What did you find?"

"Since nobody there would talk to me, I got a proxy to ask around. Somebody saw a gold 80s Buick pulling off the hill around the time Pa was shot. Three cars of that description exist in Black Florin."

"The owners?"

Ross opened his briefcase, removed an envelope and began laying pictures on Roman's desk. "We got Johnson Johnson–yes, that's his real name. Forty-five, truck driver. He was out in California, and his car was at Terry's Auto getting the transmission fixed–or broken, if you ask Rebel. I'm ruling him out."

Roman nodded, pushing the picture of Johnson Johnson aside to take the next.

"This is Eleanora Mabel. Her husband died some weeks ago–heart failure. I'm liable to think she pestered the man to death. She was at church the night Pa died."

Roman tossed Eleanora Mabel on top of Johnson Johnson.

"Which leaves us with the third suspect," said Ross slowly. "Another woman."

Roman held out his hand for the picture, but Ross hesitated.

"What?" Roman said.

Ross frowned. "Ah... Well, nothing."

"What?"

Ross handed him the picture.

A cold sweat broke out on Roman's neck. He handed it back.

"No," he said.

"I went to her house," Ross said. "Gold coupe in the driveway. Her name's Julette Dimple, age seventy-three. I'm told she's a regular at their church. Never misses a service. But she wasn't there that night. Eleanora Mabel confirmed it, and so did two other people."

"So this little old church lady blew off Pa's head with a shotgun? Be serious. That coupe proves nothing," said Roman. His heart was pounding.

"I hear you, but I still think I'm going to bring her in for questioning. You yourself said you suspect a woman did it."

"Leave her be, Ross."

Ross stared at him. "Roman, if she killed Pa–"

"I don't care. She's not the one."

Anger clouded his little brother's eyes. "Everybody's saying Rebel did it, and now here's proof he didn't."

"It ain't proof to me."

"Would Rebel think so?"

"Since when is Rebel any concern of yours?" Roman threw back. Ross and Rebel hated each other.

"Rebel is an illiterate jackass," said Ross curtly. "But he's our brother. Family. I don't know who that woman is to you, Roman, but..." Ross saw his older brother's look and wisely changed course. He understood there were some things about Roman's past that must never be mentioned.

"You know Pa deserved worse than a bullet," Roman said.

“Don’t you want to find out who did it?”

“Not so much anymore. I’m thinking maybe we ought to let the fucker rot in peace.” Roman scowled and picked up the picture of Julette Dimple again, put it down.

Ross said, “He was my father, too.”

“He spoiled you because he wanted your mother’s money,” said Roman bluntly. “And once that didn’t pan out, he started treating you like he treated the rest of us. Only we didn’t have no rich granny to get us out before it got too bad. What you remember is a pretense. He was a psychopath, and before he died he’d planned to take that little woman you had in Rowanville and do her what he did to Rebel’s.”

Ross’s eyes went tight.

“Look, I really called you here to ask about the girl,” said Roman.

“Your jailbait?”

Ross could have his jokes as long as he did what Roman wanted. “I want you to get her birth certificates, documents. She’s got none.” Roman opened his desk and handed a Ross a folder of everything he knew about Serena, typed and printed. Ross flipped through it with a thumb, curious in spite of his annoyance.

“She has a kid?”

“Yeah. It’s all in there.”

“Where did you find her? The street?”

“Can you do it or not?”

"Yeah, I can do it."

"Thanks."

"Well, I'm off then. If that's all you need." Ross snatched up his jacket. Roman forced his irritation aside and inspected his little brother with a close eye. Ross seemed wired, jittery. Roman suspected his brother's little snit had nothing to do with him at all. Was he really so upset about Pa's death? Or was it something else in his personal life?

"How is Tina?" Roman asked cautiously.

"She's gone," said Ross, snapping shut his briefcase. His face twisted in pain. Roman knew Ross had had a sweetheart in Rowanville — a black woman.

"Need to talk?"

"With you? No thanks."

"She ain't worth it, Ross."

"Is your teeny-bopper whore?"

Ross slammed out of the room. Roman got up and went after him, catching his brother on the arm before he could pass Serena in the kitchen. "One day somebody's gonna burn that adder's tongue right from your head," he told his little brother grimly.

Ross enunciated each word. "You're a hypocrite, Roman. You spent your whole life pretending to be someone you're not just to please Pa. And now he's dead, you're stepping right into his shoes. It's just hard to respect you sometimes."

“That’s the problem with the three of you,” Roman said, low enough he hoped Serena couldn’t hear. Ross’s bicep flexed hard under his fingers, but Roman tightened his grip until his little brother turned pale. “That’s the problem. Ungrateful. You, Rebel and Rain got to run off into the sunset chasin’ your dreams. I had to stay here. Doing his dirty work. I sacrificed everything for you boys. I busted my ass for this damned family, so you can sit in Rowanville eatin’ whore-durves with your fancy folk acting like you don’t stink of pig shit like the rest of us.”

“Don’t blame me because you were too pussy to stand up to him,” Ross bit out.

Roman gave an ugly laugh. “That you can look me in the eye and say that just proves my point.”

Ross jerked from his older brother’s grip and stalked out of the hall. Roman heard him accost Serena in the kitchen.

“Listenin’ at the keyhole?” he snapped.

Serena jumped at his tone. “Excuse me?”

Shit. Roman stalked after his brother.

“I didn’t hear a thing,” Serena retorted. “And I don’t like the way you’re talkin’ to me.”

“Why are you here? What’s he doing to you?” Ross demanded.

“Ross, get out,” said Roman, rounding the bend. Serena had her elbows deep in soapy water, washing dishes. The smell of baking meringue filled the kitchen. She looked mortified.

“I’m here to work,” said Serena, eyes flicking to Roman. “If I hear something while you two are screamin’ down the place, that ain’t my fault.”

“Ross,” said Roman. “Get out before you catch your ass.”

“Hillbilly shit,” said Ross, and slammed out of the house.

CHAPTER 8
SOMETHING EDIBLE

Happiness.

No more going hungry. No more losing sleep. She watched Isaiah put on weight and grow taller. Every week a white envelope appeared under the guest house front door. Inside it contained her weekly salary from Roman McCall, plus extra "for Isaiah". For the first time in her life she was making real money. She carefully put the extra cash into a separate pile under her mattress, hoping to save for Isaiah's school. Though six months now seemed too short a time, she knew she'd be well settled to get Isaiah what he needed when they left Roman's hill.

Her daily chores took nothing from her; Roman's house never got messy. She spent most of her time in his kitchen cooking. Breakfast, lunch, dinner. If Roman was out, she carefully wrapped and labeled the food to store in his deep fridge.

It was Mrs. Loving who made the brilliant suggestion to sell her baked goods at the church. Serena spent an entire weekend making caramels the way she'd done once with her Great Aunt Eulie. She wrapped them in colored wax paper and separated them into small boxes. Mrs. Loving returned from church that very Sunday with four hundred dollars cash and a list of orders for the future. Serena now had a second income, and since Roman gave her free rein in his kitchen she killed two birds with one stone, making her candies on the side while she cooked for him.

Roman had given her a credit card for groceries. Serena didn't touch it when she shopped for her little business. He stated bluntly that he didn't give a damn–even ordered her to use it–but Serena firmly refused. She had to set a limit on how much Roman did for her. She suspected she could ask him for almost anything and he would do it. She didn't want to take advantage.

Weeks passed. Isaiah and Mrs. Loving became the best of friends. To Serena, the old woman was nearer to an angel. Mrs. Loving watched the boy during the day while Serena did her chores and cooking for Roman. Sometimes she even stayed late to allow Serena time to study for the GED exams coming up in September. On weekends the three of them went out together around the mountain, and Mrs. Loving slowly drew Serena out of her shell. Serena found herself confessing everything to the old woman. For her part, Mrs. Loving was warmed by the girl's devotion to her son and her sweet nature. She promised to help Serena as much as she could.

Starting with Roman. Mrs. Loving understood what Roman saw in the girl, but their little arrangement had to stop. It was perverse. As she took on a motherly concern for Serena and the child she became more convinced. Roman was too old for little Miss Jones, too wrapped up in dangerous McCall affairs, and full of his own bitterness. She knew he cared for Isaiah, and he might even be falling in love with Serena. But if he truly loved her he would not force her to sleep with him. Mrs. Loving put these opinions to Roman in diplomatic terms.

"She's young and she's been sheltered from the world," said Mrs. Loving sternly. "She has a child that needs a father. You can't sweep the girl off her feet if you don't intend to make her a bride. It wouldn't be fair. You're giving her false hope."

"Serena knows this is just temporary. She agreed to this."

"She agreed because she had no choice," said Mrs. Loving, shaking a finger at him. "Intimacy should be saved for a marriage bed. Women get attached. Think, Roman! To Serena, you must be a dream come true. In time, she'll want more than to be your mistress. Do you want to disappoint her and the child? It would be cruel."

She saw she'd struck a chord with Roman. After that, she was certain he didn't take Serena to his bed again. Mrs. Loving was content. Serena seemed heartbroken by Roman's sudden avoidance, but Mrs. Loving knew she'd done the right thing. A young and pretty lassie like that would get over it. No sense for the poor girl to hang her hat on Roman. Mrs. Loving adored the man, but he was a still a mercenary. And his unnatural obsession with Serena didn't seem quite holy to Mrs. Loving. Their little affair was already making waves of gossip around the mountain.

Serena didn't know about any gossip. She lived in her own small world once again, but it was a happy world. Every night she took Isaiah on walks around the hill. When the sun went down hundreds of lightning bugs came out to waltz among the grove of apple trees lower down near the road. Near that ran a stream full of tiny fish that looked like drops of silver come to life. Following that led her and Isaiah to an old white oak. Its branches bowed under the weight of colored glass bottles, and the music they made was sad and lonesome. A lot of bees hung around the little glade there, too. Isaiah did not like this part of the walk, but Serena felt drawn to it because Mister Roman had clearly put the bottle tree there. She didn't know why, and she couldn't summon the courage to ask him. She wondered what haints he wanted to keep out of his hill.

In fact, Serena wondered quite a lot about Mister Roman. She wondered while she washed the dishes, she wondered while she piled his laundry into the machine (she definitely didn't think about smelling his shirts, ever) and she wondered while she lay alone in bed, wondering, wondering, why he didn't want to make love to her anymore.

She had it bad for Mister Roman. Yes, she did. No matter how many stern talking-tos she gave herself, let her catch sight of the man and it was over.

And when he touched her? All day long her heart spun around, her throat felt tight. It was nothing like the other times, but still. A brush on the waist here. A squeeze there.

Just take me to bed again, she wanted to beg him. *Make this stop. Make me stop wanting you.*

One time, while she was washing dishes, he came up behind her quiet as a cat. His hands circled her waist. Soapy water sloshed over her front as she automatically came to tiptoes. What should she do? She was afraid to move. The warmth of his body enveloped her. The buckle on his belt pressed into her lower back. He smelled like something edible.

"Mister Roman? Do you need something?"

"No."

Say something.

"I made another pie."

"Thank you."

"My singing bothering you?"

Now he played with the ends of her hair. "No. I liked it."

Her ass pushed back into his crotch in a slow grind. His turn to freeze. And then one of his hands crept over her stomach and guided her backward, into him. She twitched her ass again. He braced the other hand on the counter.

He's hard.

"Mister Roman," she whispered, removing her hands from the soapy water. "Maybe we could–"

The spell shattered. He backed away immediately. She turned in confusion as he left the room, rubbing the back of his neck and muttering to himself.

Roman knew he was a fool.

He avoided Serena, but traces of her now lingered everywhere. His fridge organized and labeled, hot food on the table, his clothes pressed, porch swept, the rooms of the house aired out and steadily filling with plants. He suspected Mrs. Loving's hand in that and confirmed those suspicions when he saw her and Serena sneaking in the back door with pots of orchids.

Orchids.

"They'll die," he told Serena gruffly. "These things don't grow well."

"You'll see," she said, loosening up the roots carefully with her bare hands. She said, "People think growing orchids is like rocket science. It's all about leaving 'em to do their thing and giving a little boost of confidence now and then." She held up the pot. A delicate yellow flower bobbed in his face. "Pretty, right?"

"I guess."

"Put it up there on that shelf. The windows in here are so big you don't have to worry about light. It'll get enough."

He did as she requested. "You'd need a ladder to get up there, Serena."

"No, I don't."

"How will you water it?"

"I ain't gonna water that one. That's yours."

He narrowed his eyes. "I look like an orchid-tender? You bought the damn thing, you take care of it."

She smiled. "I just want to prove you wrong. You think you can't keep a little plant alive, I'll show you that you can."

He'd never know where the hell she learned about orchids. Serena had a deeply curious mind. During the grand tour

Roman hadn't bothered showing her the library, eager to get his pretty new toy in bed and convinced a girl like that wouldn't cotton to books, anyway.

Well, he was dead wrong. Serena was a bandit in that library. Empty spaces opened up on the shelves and refilled in a matter of days. She stayed up late to read. The light in her bedroom flicked off only a few hours before dawn, and somehow she timed herself to his own insomniac schedule so he always woke with a hot biscuit, sausage gravy and a bowl of fruit sitting on the table. She poured him coffee straight from the pot, yawning into the back of her hand.

"Up too late with them books," he grunted one morning after thinking hard for something to say that wouldn't make her jump and stammer. They had lost some of their earlier intimacy. His fault. Mrs. Loving's reproach, plus Ross's slick remarks, made him reconsider everything. Now he kept his distance, except for those moments of weakness...

Right. The books. "You didn't say nothing about the library. I put 'em back when I'm done," she said.

Roman took her hand and opened it palm up on the table. He rubbed his thumb over her calluses. "Do you like it here?" he asked in a low voice.

"Yes, I like it," she said.

"And your boy?"

"He's very happy."

"If you need something, you tell me right away."

"I will. Thank you." She swallowed hard and then curled her fingers around his. "W-what about you? If there's something you need..."

He took his hand away. "Don't."

"Why?" she said, her beautiful eyes swimming in his vision.

"We can't. It ain't right."

She got up and sat in his lap. Her thighs dimpled under his grip and her tits heaved a kissing distance from his mouth. She smelled like cinnamon tea.

"Serena, get off me."

"What if this is what I need?" she whispered.

"You're a child. This ain't what you need. It was wrong. It was a mistake."

"But–"

His voice became steel. "I said, get off."

She slid back into her chair. Her humiliated expression hurt worse than the silence after.

Thoughts of Serena tangled up in his brain, twisted and sick.

Serena riding his dick.

Serena sucking his dick.

Serena underneath him, creamy and tight, struggling to take him deeper.

"Relax," Junie purred, kneeling down and unbuckling his belt. He closed his eyes and shifted his ass deeper into the velvet couch. The woman plucked at his fly, her long fake nails clicking together.

He swore the honky-tonk wail in the barroom downstairs was the same he'd been hearing all night. He wished he could shoot out the damn speakers. These greasy places had the worst fucking taste.

He grunted as the woman flicked her tongue under his cockhead. *Just do it and leave. One quick nut and it's done.*

"What the hell?" said Junie.

He opened his eyes. He had his hand on her head, the muscles of his entire arm straining as he held her away from him like a man trying to stop an overeager spaniel from nipping at his cuffs.

"You don't want it?" she blinked.

Do it, or you're gonna fuck that girl in your house until she hates you.

"Naw," he said, the words coming out like broken glass. "Naw, guess I don't."

"Talk to me, baby," she pouted.

"I ain't your baby, Junie." He reached for his belt. "Forget it. Money's over there."

"Is it that darkie girl that got you so wound up?" Junie said, lifting her chin. Word spread like wildfire that Roman was keeping Bubba's baby mama as a live-in whore after snatching her from right under Curley's nose.

"No." He snapped his belt shut. "Get me a drink."

"Asshole." She slammed out of the room.

Roman rubbed his pounding temples. He had to get the fuck out of here. Leaving Junie at the bar, he stepped outside and ran slap bang into his brother Rain.

"Watch where the fuck you're stepping," slurred Rain. "You son of a–aw, shit. Roman?"

And so the night went from bad to worse. Rain looked like something that had crawled out of a gutter. He stank. He wobbled as if the hooch bottle he held between forefinger and thumb overbalanced him.

"You high?" Roman snarled, catching Rain by the collar.

"Nope," said Rain. "Just drunk."

"Where the fuck have you been?"

"Drinking."

"I mean for the last four months."

"Quit yellin' in my face." Rain wiped his mouth. "I'm sorry, alright?"

"Sorry for what? Making us think you were fucking dead?" Roman shoved him.

"Maybe I was dead. Felt like it."

"The name Terry ring any bells? Six thousand dollars?"

"No," Rain lied, backing away from him.

Roman slapped him. His brother stumbled back, eyes flying wide. He bared his teeth at Roman like a wild animal. “Fuck, you asshole.”

“Don’t fucking lie to me, Rain. I’ve been goin’ crazy trying to track your sorry ass down. Not knowing if you were dead– When was the last time you saw a real bed? Where you staying at?”

“Shh. Look, I got these, Roman.” Rain pulled a baggie of blue pills from his pocket and shook it. His fingernails were filthy. “See? These little bastards take it all away. All the bullshit in here. All the *noise*.” He screwed a finger into his forehead. “Maybe you could use some. Loosen you up so you can get the stick out your ass.”

Roman made a grab for the bag but somehow his drunk, high little brother was faster. Rain shoved the drugs back into his pocket. “Get your own.”

“Who sold you that?”

“None of your goddamn business.”

“Rain, just quit it. Please,”

“Why? It makes me happy. Ain’t that what we all want? Just some happiness before it all goes up in smoke. BANG! Nothing left.” Rain laughed and laughed. He threw the bottle of hooch at the ground so hard it exploded. Glass went everywhere.

Roman grabbed Rain by the shirt. “You’re breaking my heart.”

“You don’t have one of those,” said Rain. He jerked from Roman’s grip and vanished into the bar.

. . .

An hour later Roman returned to his hill. The light in Serena's bedroom drew him like a moth to the killing flame.

"Mister Roman?" she opened the door at his first knock. She wore a white nightie, her hair wrapped in a piece of satin which she snatched off her head the moment he turned his back.

"Where's the boy?" he grunted, stepping inside. He hung his stetson on the coat rack and jacked off his dirty boots.

"In bed. It's *midnight*."

"Right."

He stalked past her into the living room. Serena kept the guest house neat as a pin, everything in its place, just the way he liked it. Her warm-cinnamon-sugar smell couldn't have been more welcome after the smoky stink of the bar.

One good thing among this bullshit.

"Where have you been?" she asked. "You got that smell on you again. Whiskey and cigarettes." She leaned forward and sniffed him. Her eyes flashed. "You saw a woman?"

Where have I been? Trying to get you out of my head.

"Nevermind," she said, turning away. "I don't want to know."

The guest house came with a fully stocked liquor cabinet. Roman took a pitcher of sweet tea from the fridge, poured it into two glasses and topped them off with a finger of gin each. He handed her one. She took it from him and immediately set it down on the countertop.

"You been avoiding me," she said.

"I have," he admitted.

"Why? I thought..." She bit her lip, falling back on anger to avoid being vulnerable. "Who were you with tonight? Her funky ass perfume is all over you."

"Just an old friend." He wouldn't even call Junie that. Roman shook his head. "It was a mistake. I knew that right away."

"You said you wouldn't have other women."

"I got needs like any man, Serena."

"You were fine with me until a few weeks ago. If you don't want me anymore then say it, but I know that's not true. I know you want me, Roman. I'm right here–I'm willing." She swallowed. "How pathetic is that? I'm begging you to be with me."

Roman looked up at the ceiling. He'd asked for this fight by coming here, but it didn't make it easier. "Serena, trust me, it ain't that I don't want you. All the time I'm thinking about you... Every day, every hour, I'm doing things to forget you."

"Then why?"

"It's trouble. You're trouble for me."

"Maybe I should go out and find some man to do what you won't," she said recklessly. His eyes snapped open. "Then you'd be out on your ass," he snarled. "I don't share, girl."

"Either you want me or you don't! You can't have it both ways." Her eyelids lowered, the thick lashes veiling the simmering rage beneath. "Did you fuck that woman?"

"No. Nothing happened."

"Okay."

"I don't lie, Serena. If I slept with somebody else I would admit it right now. But I didn't. I couldn't, knowing that you–" he broke off, the words clotting in his throat. He swore. "Hell, you know why I'm here. It ain't easy for a man like me to admit these things. I can't talk about my feelings and all that shit."

"That's why I'm here. That's what you're paying me for. Anything you need from me, you can get it."

"Maybe that's just it," said Roman hoarsely.

She frowned, unsure what he meant. She sidled closer to him. "Just tell me why you stopped. I wanted to wear these pretty drawers for you. I wanted to sleep with you."

"Only because I paid you."

"I never had a man touch me the way you touch me," she whispered. "It ain't about the money."

"Shit," he said.

She took his hand and rested it on her stomach. He clutched a handful of silky fabric. He bent his head. Her mouth opened under his, sweet as a flower. He tasted her nectar. He bit and sucked on her soft, thick lips. She pulled back first, her eyes swirling with desire.

"The bedroom," she whispered.

He hoisted her into his arms and quietly kicked open her bedroom door. She grabbed him by the belt loops and sat down hard on the end of the bed.

The nightie slipped off her shoulders; she bared her breasts. There was something dangerously erotic about having a naked woman squirming underneath him while he was dressed. Feeling like a king about to despoil some innocent virgin, he rolled the nightie up and stroked her bare pussy. *I'll just touch her here. Just for a minute... Nothing more.*

She rolled her hips like an exotic dancer, sliding onto his long fingers and leaving a trail of sweet cream. *Fuck it.* He nudged her knees apart.

As his tongue slid inside her, she arched underneath him and stifled a cry in the back of her hand. Roman grabbed her broad hips and held her down as he buried his face in her cunt, parting her pussy lips and laying the flat of his tongue down for long, tasting strokes. Her clit plumped up, and he went there next, hard and slow, light and teasing...

"Roman," she gasped, her small hand slamming on the back of his head, tightening in the new crop of curly hair.

So *tight*. He worked his middle finger deep, fucking her down to his first knuckle while he sucked the aching knot of her clit. She came apart in a wave of tremors and half-strangled cries.

Time passed in a haze. He loved eating pussy, never got to do it, and Serena was just perfect. He caressed her thick thighs and childbearing hips as his brain went wild with dark fantasies. She had one of those puffy, tight pussies that made men wild.

"Shit. Hold on, hold on," he muttered. *Slow down.* He raised himself up on the bed, knee sinking into the mattress beside her. He stroked her stomach under the nightie as she came down like a feather in the air, all a-shiver. The ridges of her stretch marks bumped against his fingertips.

"Serena. Babygirl. I–"

"Ma?"'

They leapt apart like rabbits. Serena shoved the nightie down and hauled the straps over her shoulders. "Isaiah! What–what's wrong, baby?" she stammered.

"Who's that?" Isaiah whispered from the door.

"Uh–It's just Mister Roman," said Serena, fumbling for the light. Roman hastily stowed his dick away and backed up from the bed. Isaiah glared daggers at him when the light flicked on. "Why's he here?" the boy demanded sleepily.

"He's just leaving," said Serena, glancing up at Roman. "Right?"

"Uh-huh. Yeah." He cleared his throat. "Sorry, little man."

Isaiah gave him a shrewd look that made Roman have to forcibly restrain a laugh.

"What were you doing, Ma?"

"Um, Mister Roman was telling me a story," said Serena quickly. Roman made a very un-Roman noise. Serena's lips twitched. She turned her laugh into a cough and gently herded Isaiah from the room.

CHAPTER 9

CRAZY GOOD

Roman drove to Green Tree hill in the early hours of dawn. By the time the sun rose to mid-sky, sweat plastered his shirt to his shoulders and twelve inches of dried mud stiffened the cuffs of his Wranglers. He could barely close his hands into fists after hours of clipping and cutting and sawing through thick bark. His back ached, his muscles screamed in protest, and Serena was, for now, a distant thought.

Green Tree Hill buzzed with activity. Cutters marched through rows of spiny-leafed plants that stretched as far as the eye could see. With every gust of wind, the hillside shivered as if in anticipation. Darting up and down the rows were other members of the McCall family and hired hands from Black Florin. They worked under foremen who oversaw the different sections of the hill. But every man there ultimately answered to Roman McCall, who paid their wages.

Roman took his first break in six hours with a glass of cold sweet tea. In the shade of a poplar, two older black women sold plates of brisket, beans, cornbread and slaw for seven dollars a piece. These women came to every harvest. Roman didn't know their names, but some said they were mountain witches. The tall McCall watched cutters refill their sweet tea from the pitcher at the women's table. Somehow this pitcher remained full, the floating lemons bright and yellow. The ice never melted. The tea, like the brisket, was heavenly delicious. *But Serena's is better.*

Spirits ran high. Everybody agreed that the Green Tree fields had bushed out nicely and might in fact be the greatest yield in years.

But he couldn't get his hopes up yet. A lot of daylight stretched between harvest and delivery. A lot of room for error.

And for the first time in thirty years, the harvesting of Virginia Gold Kush would happen without his father. He needed to prove himself.

Sometimes, Roman questioned if the risk of growing bud was worth it. Other criminal ops in the region didn't bother with weed anymore. The "Green Highway" drew predators from the hills like locusts to sweet corn. From the constant sabotage from rival growers, attacks from random gangs, and the DEA working overtime to be a royal pain in the ass, smuggling crop out of the hills required intense effort and planning.

Legalization bills made circles in the state government, getting nowhere, while Federales seeking promotions could always boost their rep by taking down runners. The McCalls ran a well-defended enterprise and greased the right palms, but the problem of transportation remained.

And it would remain as long as the Florin family stuck with marijuana. Roman would prefer to get rid of the fields altogether and focus on smaller businesses in town, but probably the family would rather get rid of him first. Many McCalls, especially those near the bottom of the pyramid, depended on the income from selling dope.

Roman argued it was not a reliable income. Some years the crops failed–especially with the harsher summers and freak rainstorms that seemed to come more frequently these days. That was why the Snatch Hills had been pushing for a move to harder drugs. Pills were easier to smuggle across state lines with triple the street value of weed. They didn't need a bunch of land and effort to produce, and since they were addicting, customers always returned. It was basically free money, so why did Roman McCall have a problem with it? The Snatch Hills whispered and grumbled and slowly gained support. Roman didn't care. He wasn't having that shit in his town. Ever.

As soon as he finished the tea he moved down the line of trucks. His cousin Saverin approached, slapping the sweat from his mesh-back.

Since Roman's three younger brothers had abandoned the business, Roman had been grooming one of the Bailey boys to be his right hand. Saverin, brother of Sam, actually bore a passing resemblance to Roman. Sam was ruddy, like Ross, while Saverin had black hair and a hawkish face.

"How goes it, cuz?" Saverin asked.

"It goes. Good harvest."

"Good harvest," Saverin agreed. He lowered his voice. "Heard about the job you did with Sam."

Roman nodded. “I didn’t know the man.”

“I bet you it was the Snatch Hills what sent him.”

“Can’t prove it,” Roman shrugged.

Saverin wiped his forehead on the back of his wrist. “I swear I did the work of ten men today.” He pointed down the hill with his chin. “Mind you, Gump’s gone for water about six times this half hour.”

Gumperson Green Tree stood under the barn house, fanning his red face. “It’s my blood sugar,” he informed anybody who would listen. “Can’t do nothing when my sugar’s like this.”

When Gump saw Roman’s narrow black eyes trained on him, he hastily trotted out of sight.

“Duke would have busted his teeth in,” Saverin remarked.

“Don’t know if I can afford to piss off the Green Trees,” Roman admitted to his cousin. “They could make trouble if they stopped scratching their asses and banded with the Snatch Hills. Folks like ‘em. Plus they got that nephew in the government.”

“You worried about the government?”

“Feds get froggier every year. I like my freedom.”

“Especially now that Duke’s dead,” Saverin said. He flushed. “Hell, I didn’t mean it like that. I know he was your Daddy. But you two was always fang and claw. Any update on who killed him? Everybody says it was Rebel’s doing.”

“Rebel didn’t do it,” said Roman. “That I can say.”

"There's many who'd like to see the man caught. I just can't believe nobody saw nothing. Shot down like a dog. Imagine that."

Many people shared Saverin's disbelief. Duke was a living icon, a Man of Florin. He paid for weddings, funerals, baseball fields, and scholarships. His funeral drew a crowd so large it had deadlocked traffic in every corner of the mountain. Even folks from the back hills came to pay their dues, laying gnarled and filthy hands on the stark white casket lid. Closed casket. The shotgun that took Duke's life had also blown his head off.

And now the "gypsy" had taken up the reins. To be sure, uniting the bickering McCall clans under one flag could not happen overnight. Mountain people respected strength, which Roman had without question. But his blood made him a suspicious figure as much as his introverted nature.

Roman needed no more stains on his reputation. He'd always been a private man, a lone wolf with a murky history. People gave him the benefit of the doubt as Duke's firstborn son and acknowledged heir–though like Duke himself, they would have preferred Rebel, to take up the latter title.

Nothing would cement his popularity more than a successful harvest.

"So what's with that girl you stole from Curley?" asked Saverin. He happened to say it in front of two black cutters. The men exchanged looks but swiftly glanced away as if they hadn't heard a thing.

"I hired her for a maid. That's all there is to say. She weren't Curley's to begin with," Roman said shortly.

"You fucking her?"

"No." It was half true. He hadn't fucked Serena. Yet.

Saverin shook his head. "Y'all and those women. First Ross, then Rebel, then Rain..."

Roman's ears perked up. "What about Rain?"

"I heard he got a yellow girl he's seeing down in Rowanville," replied Saverin.

"Probably his drug dealer," Roman dismissed.

"Yeah, probably." Sav rubbed his jaw, his eyes dancing with mischief. "So you and Curley's woman..."

"She ain't Curley's, I said."

"I heard she's got a kid and everything. Bubba's kid."

"You Baileys gossip like females."

The amusement left Saverin's voice. He frowned in concern. "Just so you know, the Uncles ain't happy about it," he said.

"They're never happy," Roman said. Duke's brothers had never liked him. The feeling was mutual.

Gypsy. Bad seed. Roman kneaded a hard knot behind his neck. "Times change," he added.

"Uh huh." Saverin eyed him sideways. "We tolerate the darkies, but maybe that's as far as it should go. They got their own agenda and it'll bring nothing good to us."

Roman grunted.

"It's a fact." Saverin spat tobacco juice in a long arc. "Look at 'em. Look at how they live. They're parasites, and our taxes support 'em. We ought to cut 'em all loose. Shit, you used to say the same yourself."

Sav spoke true. Hell, Roman called Rebel every name in the book for getting friendly with the doll-faced woman on Grace Hill.

"Stop messin', Roman," Sav urged. "Give the girl back to Curley and call it square. It ain't worth losing the Snatch Hills over."

Roman eyed his cousin. "You scared of 'em or something?"

"No," said Saverin quickly. "But Curley's talkin' shit. Sayin' you and Rebel will turn the clan over to the niggers. Saying how you got 'dirty blood'. "

"I don't like that word, Saverin."

His cousin laughed. "Right."

"I mean it."

Saverin stopped laughing. "You serious?"

"Yeah, I am."

They stared at each other. Saverin Bailey shook his head. "You really have changed."

"Change is good sometimes," said Roman. "And maybe I do got dirty blood, but surely no more than the rest of you inbreds." His eyes flickered. "Can you do something for me,?"

"Sure. What you need?" said Saverin instantly. *Loyal as a Bailey*, the saying went.

"Get a message to Curley," Roman said. "You can send it through your Snatch Hill cousins. Tell him if he wants the girl so bad, he can fight me one-on-one. I'll give him a fair shake. If Curley can beat my ass, I'll hand the girl over."

"I'd give my left nut for a front-row seat to that."

A smile ghosted on Roman's lips. "Is that Gump down there asleep?" he wondered.

Saverin followed his gaze. *Lazy as a Green Tree*, went another saying. "It is, Roman," Saverin confirmed.

"To hell with diplomacy. Go wake the bastard up."

"Gladly." Grinning, Saverin jogged down the hill.

"Yes, right there."

Serena's hands worked down his back, the oil guiding her firm fingers over the contours of his knotted muscles. Down the hall, the TV's flickering light reflected on the wall. From the silence, they could tell Isaiah still slept soundly. Thank God. The boy lay nuzzled under a blanket in the living room, Dinosaur clutched tightly in his little fist.

Serena dug her knuckles into Roman's lower back and he buried a manly scream into his wrist. She chuckled softly. "There?"

"Yes. God."

She massaged him, using her body weight to press deep. Getting to touch Roman's powerful body excited her. "Aren't you glad about those rabbits?" She teased.

An hour before Serena had said goodbye to Mrs. Loving goodbye and taken Isaiah for a walk. They spent the twilight hours looking at a nest of rabbits under a hydrangea bush.

"Will Mister Roman keep them?" he asked Serena anxiously as they returned home.

"They aren't pets, Isie."

"Why not?"

"Rabbits can be a pest sometimes. Eating vegetables and flowers. They're wild animals."

She would never know how the next thought entered Isaiah's head. "Will he kill them, Ma?" her son asked fearfully.

"No, baby. I'm sure he won't."

"But what if he kills them? And make them into stew? Like this book Mrs. Loving showed me, they was eating rabbit stew."

"Isaiah, nobody is gonna hurt them rabbits."

"Can we take them inside to save them? What if it rains?"

"No, Isaiah. I told you they ain't pets."

Isaiah was relentless. "But what if we took them inside? They could live in my room."

"No, Isaiah."

"Why not, Ma? Please?"

Isaiah cried, and Serena struggled to calm him down, feeling both amused and exasperated at Isaiah's insistence that the rabbits would for sure be turned into stew if he didn't invite them to come live under his bed. The guest house phone rang. She gingerly picked up the receiver, rubbing Isaiah's fluffy head to comfort him.

"Hello?"

"Serena," came Roman's dry voice. "Are you murdering that child?"

"He's upset about the rabbits."

"The what?"

Serena explained. Roman said, "Bring the boy up here. I'll talk to him."

After hanging up she got Isaiah to calm down enough to dress him presentable and wash his face. They took the short walk up the hill and let themselves into Roman's house. She didn't find Roman in the living room, nor in the kitchen. A trail of mud and grass led to the main hallway. She led Isaiah to Roman's bedroom. "Mister Roman will promise not to hurt the rabbits, okay? So you better stop with all this carrying on."

"What if he doesn't?" Isaiah whispered.

"Then I'll hit him with my shoe."

Isaiah didn't even crack a smile. *I'll get him a pet someday,* Serena promised herself silently. *Once we get settled somewhere more permanent. A cat would be nice.*

She pushed open Roman's bedroom door. To her surprise, Roman lay spread-eagled and facedown on his bed. He looked dead.

"Are you alright?" she cried.

"Fine," Roman grunted without moving an inch. "Where's the boy?"

Isaiah shuffled to Roman's bedside. He knuckled away his tears before he spoke, but his small voice still shook. "Mister Roman, will you promise not to kill the rabbits? The rabbits under the hydration bush. There's a mommy and three babies. I want them to live in my bedroom," he said in a rush.

"What did your Ma say?" Roman asked.

"She said no," said Isaiah.

"Your Ma knows best. A wild animal's meant for the wild. You got to let nature take its course."

"But you helped me and Ma leave our old house and now I want to help the rabbits," reasoned Isaiah.

"It's a little different from that, son."

Son. Serena's heart flipped over. *Don't read into it.*

"Lots of other animals eat rabbits–and they got babies to feed too, don't they? It's hard, 'cause those bunnies are cute, but we can't let our feelings get in the way of how nature's supposed to work. At least not with animals. People? Now that's different." Roman's voice was muffled in the pillow.

"Why?" Isaiah scowled. "Why is it different?"

"Isaiah," said Serena, getting worried that Roman had somehow paralyzed himself.

"It just is," said Roman. "It's the way God made it. Now the best I can do is promise not to cook those rabbits into stew. You ever had rabbit stew, Isaiah?"

"No," said Isaiah vehemently. "I'll never, ever eat rabbits."

"You're missin' out. But you know what? I'll tell the gardener about them rabbits, and he'll keep an eye out."

"Ma says the gardener is an old drunk."

"*Isaiah*."

Roman huffed a laugh. Then he groaned.

"Are you alright?" Serena asked, moving closer.

"I'm fine," Roman said unconvincingly. He moved a fraction in the bed, trying to turn towards Isaiah. "Now listen, little man, don't go giving your Ma gray hairs. Big boys don't pitch hissy fits. You can keep an eye on those rabbits, but if it's God's plan to take 'em, there's nothing you can do."

"That's not fair."

"Neither is life, son."

Son. And the word had a strange effect on Isaiah. He seemed to stand a little taller. "Okay," he said, still upset but with a lot more to think about than before.

"Good," said Roman. "Good man. Is your Ma still there?"

"Yes," replied Isaiah.

"Serena, can your boy do me a favor?"

"What?" she asked curiously.

"I need him to walk on my back."

"Is that a good idea? Are you hurt? Do you need to go to a hospital?"

Roman gave a bark of laughter which he immediately regretted. "No, I don't need no hospital. Hoist him up," he wheezed.

Isaiah took his shoes off and climbed up on Roman's back. "It's sweaty!" Isaiah exclaimed.

Quickly the rabbits were forgotten. Isaiah wobbled up and down Roman's broad shoulders, his shy giggles warming Serena's heart. There was a sick popping noise and Roman groaned again. "Yeah. That's it."

"Do you want me to go down?" Isaiah asked.

"Yeah. Lower."

The moment Isaiah's foot touched Roman's lower back the big man let out a bellow that sent Isaiah in a startled topple to the bed. Both of them started laughing, though Roman's laugh turned into a kind of strangled panting.

"Okay, that's enough," Serena said, scooping Isaiah away. She stared down at the immobile Roman McCall. His T-shirt lay damp against his shoulders, streaked with brown earthy stains. The jeans were in worse shape, and he still wore his working boots. He must have come straight into the room and collapsed across the bed. For a man as obsessively clean as Roman it showed how much pain he was in.

"You sure you're alright?" She asked worriedly.

"Yeah. Go on–watch TV with the boy or whatever. I'll be out in a while."

She hesitated, then gently touched his forehead where the black curls lay in damp ringlets. "You want tea or something?"

"Women. Y'all think tea will solve everything."

"How about a kick in the butt?" she said sweetly.

"I could be into that," he mumbled. She snorted and led Isaiah out of the room.

"Ma?" said Isaiah sleepily, an hour later. "Do you like Mister Roman?"

"He's a nice man."

"Do you like him more than Mrs. Loving?"

"I like them the same, but in different ways," Serena said carefully, stroking his head. *Please don't ask about the other night.*

"I was afraid of him, but I'm not anymore," said Isaiah.

"That's good. He's a nice man."

"Mrs. Loving says he can't be my Pa."

"She's right. Don't be worrying about that, Isaiah. We'll be just fine, like the rabbits."

Isaiah drifted off. His quiet snores lulled Serena herself. She stared at the muted movie playing on the TV, stroking Isaiah's fluffy head and thinking about what a sensitive, gentle boy he was. Not too sensitive, she hoped. A hard road lay ahead of her and Isaiah, and she needed him to be strong. She hoped her son would grow up to be a protector who looked out for people and didn't take nobody's bullshit.

Am I making him too soft?

She shut her eyes. She heard water running in Roman's room. Some minutes later Roman came out of the bedroom, shirtless, his hair dripping. "Serena?"

She raised her head, blinking sleepily. "You ain't dead, then."

He crossed the room. "And you stayed."

"I was worried about you."

He inclined his head towards his bedroom. "Will you come in for a minute?"

She glanced down at Isaiah. "I don't know how long he'll sleep for."

"Just a minute. The boy will bide out here. He never puts that thing down, does he?"

"Dinosaur? No. He's had it since he was a baby."

Roman's gaze softened as he stared down at Serena's son. "He's so peaceful."

"He's a sweet boy. What do you need me for?"

"To play doctor," he said with the shy smile that made him look a decade younger.

And so she found herself perched on Roman's back, rubbing a camphor salve into his muscles.

"What the hell was you doing today? Breaking stones?" she muttered.

“Cutting,” he grunted. “Must’ve pulled something. I walked in here and felt like I broke my ass. Barely made it into bed.”

Her hands glided over his meaty biceps. “How does that feel?”

“Incredible.”

“How the hell does a man get so big? What did they feed you growin’ up?”

“Everybody’s tall in my family.”

On your Mama’s side, too? But she didn’t dare ask it. With a sigh Serena laid herself out over Roman’s back, her thumbs digging between his angel bones.

“Thanks, sweetheart,” he murmured.

“You’re welcome. You got any more aches and pains? Lower down, maybe?” she teased in his ear.

“Your boy was fixing to shoot me when he caught us. I ain’t interferin’ with you again.”

“But I like when you interfere with me,” she whispered, squeezing his ass.

“Minx.”

With a wicked smile, she poked a finger into his ribs. He flinched like he’d been shot. “What the—”

“So you are ticklish. I knew it.”

“Oh, now you asked for it.” He grabbed her around the waist and bore her down to the bed.

“You’ll hurt your back again.”

Ignoring her warning, he dug his thumbs under her ribcage, "No! No, please..." she dissolved into helpless giggles. He caught her chin and kissed her. She opened her mouth, feeling the heat of his tongue sweep inside her. When Roman pulled away his dark eyes were soft, the way they got only for her. He stroked up and down her waist.

She bit her lip, guilty. "We shouldn't... Isaiah is right out there."

"We'll be quiet."

She opened her legs and his hard cock, hampered by layers of strong denim, pressed deep into her softness. She gasped. "Do that again. Wait, no. Don't."

"Shit." He rubbed himself against her like a dog. "Okay. We'll stop. We'll stop."

But she didn't want him to stop. She looped her arms over his broad shoulders. Her own heart thudded with both excitement and fear. She spread her legs wider. Roman unfastened her jeans and delved a hand into her panties.

She pressed his fingers, encouraging him to cup and squeeze her cunt. "That feels nice," she whispered.

"You got such a hot little body." Hunger leaped in his eyes. "But maybe we should stop."

She rocked her hips into his hand and told him what he wanted to hear. "Yes, we can. No, we shouldn't."

"Will you take your hair down for me?"

She reached back and wrestled with the scrunchie. Roman's own big hand came up to help her. He spread her frizzy afro out, fanning it over her shoulders, stroking and petting it like a precious thing.

"My God. Look at you," he muttered.

She wanted to feel him, too. She stroked his muscled stomach, up to his smooth, hairless, hard chest. He was just so big. Digging his hands in her hair, he bent her head back slowly, exposing her throat. "You scared?"

Delirious, she shook her head. He lowered his head and kissed right under her ear. Lower. And then he used his teeth. A whimper escaped her, and he licked the bite, sucked on it. He liked power. He liked control. And though Serena had been controlled and used by men before, with Roman it was so different. It gave her a sick pleasure to let a man like him use her; a man stronger than Bubba or Curley or anybody else. His tall, muscled body was golden and sculpted like a man's should be. He smelled like hot sunlight and ashes and leather and salt. She wasn't lying. She wanted him inside her.

Yes, God. Here was a man who could fight and protect her... A man who could kill for her. Roman would never hurt her the way the rest of them did. It felt even wickeder because he was paying her to be his private whore. Now she was his to use, his to fuck; every hole in her soft female body belonged to this giant.

I'm crazy for wanting this. But why does crazy feel so good?

Roman dragged her tank top down, baring her breasts. All the women he'd ever fucked, the small town belles with their blue eyes and limp yellow hair, didn't hold a candle to Serena. Her breasts overflowed his palms, brown and gold with ripe dark nipples. Her nipples bounced on his tongue. Roman fell backward on the bed, taking her with him, sucking and laving at the pebbled flesh in a blind, shuddering delirium. His other hand heavily groped her ass.

He'd always lusted for black women. His dirty little secret. Nobody knew; nobody's business, but in his private, filthiest fantasies, he saw a dark-skinned female with thick thighs, a juicy ass, and hair he could clench in his fist and bury his face in as he buried other parts deep. She had brown eyes, a plump pussy, and didn't smell like cheap whore's perfume. She smelled like cinnamon. She had a pretty face with a soft mouth. Serena was all those things.

She liked when he sucked her breasts; he'd remember that. She arched her back and tipped her ass up. He popped her thick dark nipple from his mouth and slid his thumbs into the elastic of her thong.

"You'll be a good girl for me?"

She nodded.

"I'm gonna fuck you now."

"Yes, Roman."

He got a Magnum from the bathroom, tossed it on the bed next to her.

"You trust me, honey?"

"I trust you."

"Open your mouth."

She swallowed his spit as it pooled on her tongue, a degrading act that marked his complete possession. And then, eyes dark with arousal, she opened her mouth for more.

"Back up on the bed," he ordered hoarsely, wiping his lips with his thumb. "Take those jeans off."

He glanced at the door. Shit. What if Isaiah woke up?

Fast. Do it fast.

She laid on her stomach and worked the offending item off. Pale cream streaked her thighs; her panties were limp with it. Roman jerked the thong up into her ass crack, watching the elastic snap back down and get trapped in her pussy lips. He unlatched his belt with shaking hands.

He shoved his own mud-stiff denim down. His thick cock bounced off her ass as he mounted her.

"You good with it like this?"

"Y-yeah."

He rolled the condom down. Everything in him wanted to fuck her bare. Their first time, and he wanted nothing between them. And maybe it wasn't right, but the thought of his seed shooting into Serena's womb made him fucking dizzy with an ungodly lust. Serena pregnant? His sweet Serena, big with his child, growing a baby they made together in this very bed, in this very moment? This was how mistakes happened, roared the rational part of himself, but he didn't care, he just wanted Serena to be his woman... to always be tied to him. He wanted to put a child inside her. His mouth was watering at the very idea, a sure sign he was a twisted bastard. He held open her pink pussy and lined it up with the blunt head of his sheathed cock, fighting the devil inside him with everything he had. He nailed her to the bed.

Serena gasped. A small, sharp inhale. And then her body began to shake.

And shake.

She was coming.

"Oh darlin'," he bowed the top of his head to the back of hers, and his laugh of disbelief was almost hopeless too. He'd lost it for real. No way he was ever, ever giving this up. Serena would be his. Forever.

He pressed her into the bed and fucked her.

She couldn't breathe or think.

Roman wrapped his arms around her from above. He just held her down and fucked her until she heard her own arousal like wet and sticky slapping. The secret place inside her that no man ever touched accepted him. Deeper. He went deeper. He was going to break her in half with that big thick dick.

Do it. Break me. She'd never felt so aroused and desperate. What was happening? Her thighs clenched around his hips.

"I'm gonna fucking blow," he gritted. "It's going all over your ass."

But first, she splashed her arousal all over his sheets. Roman slipped out of her pussy and took the condom off. He came endlessly over Serena, thick jets of his seed that slipped down over the seam of her pussy lips in hot trails. He flipped her over and spent the rest on her tits and stomach, shuddering through each wave of his orgasm, one hand holding her firmly in place to receive it. Pearly white ropes of semen gleamed on her skin. His eyes burned possessively, the hand stroking himself slowed. Roman rubbed his sperm into her skin with his thumb.

He still wore his muddy work jeans halfway up his ass. The hair around his dick was damp, curly, and stained by her woman's arousal. Sweat glistened on his broad chest. He looked down at her curvaceous figure splattered with his cum. A hand the size of a cast iron pan fondled her hips.

"Put it back inside," she whispered.

He thumbed a smear of cum from his dick. Then he levered her legs on his shoulders and slid inside her again. He was hard as granite, like he hadn't just blown a full load over her ass and breasts.

"It's like you got b-bigger. Roman!" Her next cry was lost to the inside of his palm. Tears of joy ran down her cheeks. Roman's hips thudded into hers. He leaned down and spoke right into her ear while his cock made a sticky mess between her legs.

"Serena," He said. *Thrust. Thrust. Thrust.*

"Y-yes."

Thrust. "You a good girl?"

"Yes. For you."

"Good girls take it all the way." She squirmed, trying to adjust to his size in this new position. "I'm good. I'm good," she whispered.

"Yes, you are. You're the best." His eyes watered for a moment. "Shit."

She gasped and hugged him around the neck, sobbing as he thrust deeper and harder. He was so deep now he could barely rock his hips. This was intimate. Scary.

"Never leave," he said, clutching her close.

"Roman..."

"I'll drag you back, you understand?"

"I won't," she mumbled, pushing the black curls off his forehead.

He pulled out and came all over her stomach. Again. Sweat and seed. "Fuck. Fuck, babe..."

She grabbed her tits and smeared his cum all over her body. He collapsed in the bed and hauled her against his chest, her legs splayed over his. His cock twitched, spilling more cum onto his stomach. He made a noise as if he was in pain– like she was the one who had hurt him. And then he leaned over her, bit her neck, reached a long hand down and buried his fingers in her pussy. Three of them. And she was so wet she just opened her legs and took it. He fingered her until she sprayed over him again, jerking and clenching her teeth to stop herself from hollering like a wildcat.

After, they lay there in the wet, fucked-up sheets and didn't move. Roman covered his eyes with one hand.

"I got to put Isaiah to bed," Serena whispered. Her throat was sore.

"Right," he said.

“I would stay, but...”

He lifted the hand covering his eyes and smiled at her mischievously. Roman smiling was rare. She felt a sizzle of something sweet and secret run through her. She smiled back.

“How’s your back?” she asked.

Now he fully grinned. “Terrible.”

Laughing, she kissed his cheek. “Good night, big man.”

He caught her hand and twined her fingers in his. “Shower in here. I’ll listen out for the boy.”

She kissed his nose. “Okay. Thank you.”

“You missed a spot,” he teased.

“That’s for next time,” she whispered.

CHAPTER 10
UGLY WORDS

"He's got that girl in there living like a slave."

"Uh huh, that's what I heard."

"You remember Felicia? With the yellow eyes? That's her baby girl."

"Is Felicia the one who killed that man?"

"Uh-huh. Rayvaughn's sister."

"Rayvaughn with the gold tooth?"

"That's the one."

"I remember Felicia. Pretty gal. Whorish. I ain't surprised about the daughter."

"You know that's right."

"What's happenin' to these girls, Eleanora?"

"I wish I knew. I guess most of 'em just want that white man's money. But that one? That lil' girl? She only care about one thing and I won't say what."

“Hee hee.”

“She was giving it to a whole football team of McCalls ‘fore she became that man’s good time. Mind you, this is the same Roman McCall who–”

“Shh, girl! There she is.”

The ladies had rounded the corner and spotted the target of their gossip. Face burning, Serena kept her gaze fixated on the cereal boxes as if she hadn’t heard a single word.

“Babylon,” the thinner woman said as they clicked past her. Her friend snickered.

Oh, hell no.

As Serena turned to give these gossiping church hens a piece of her mind, Roman appeared at the opposite end of the aisle. He passed the women straight, though both took huge steps sideways out of his way.

“You almost done?” Roman asked, oblivious to the scorching gossip he’d just interrupted. He took the shopping list from Serena’s trembling hand. She glared at the old women until they turned around, tittering to themselves.

Roman read off the list. “What’s left? Eggs? We got those in my fridge... Butter, uh-huh...” He looked up. “What’s the matter?”

“Nothing,” said Serena, forcing a smile.

“It’s damned crowded.” Roman crumpled the list and took the cart from her. “You can go wait by the car.”

“Roman?”

A fourth person swerved into the cereal aisle and instantly the church ladies reversed course and went back to a scientific examination of the granola bar boxes. A short, curvy black woman in a green dress and kitten heels clacked towards Roman and Serena. The woman had a mole under her eye. Roman froze, staring at this stranger like she was some unearthly demon bent on destroying him. Serena's suspicions reared. They clearly knew each other.

"Minnie," hailed one of the old ladies, her eyes sparkling in glee. "Hello, baby girl."

The new woman plastered a smile on her face. "Hello, Mrs. Mabel. Nice to see you."

"Mm-hmm. How's your boyfriend?"

"My *fiancé* is doing well, Mrs. Mabel. Thank you for asking. Roman, I need to speak with you *right now*."

"Let's go," said Roman, catching Serena's elbow with a little more force than was necessary.

But Serena planted her feet. If Roman was keeping another woman somewhere, and if she looked like *that*? Her stomach turned over.

The woman named Minnie halted right in front of them, her eyes darting from Roman to Serena and back again. She turned to Serena first. "Hi, honey. My name is Minnie Brown. I'm engaged to his brother, Rebel. We haven't met before."

Serena quickly recovered from her shock, giving the woman her iciest smile. "I don't think Roman ever mentioned you."

"That isn't surprising," said Minnie, glaring at Roman.

“What do you want?” Roman demanded, edging in front of Serena like the woman was dangerous.

Minnie looked over her shoulder at their audience before she replied in a low voice, “Is this the young lady who’s living with you?”

“Yes. And what?”

Minnie gave him a withering look, but when she turned back to Serena her doe-eyes softened, catching the girl off guard with the kindness she saw inside them. Minnie said, “You should know me and Rebel live just over the hill from you two. I wish we could have met sooner–”

“She ain’t a prisoner. You don’t have to do all that,” Roman interrupted angrily.

Minnie flared. “You have some nerve, Roman. Everybody is talking about what you did. If you had a decent bone in your body, you would leave this young lady alone and send her back to her people.”

Serena opened her mouth to reply, but Roman was faster. “What people?” He said harshly. “The degenerates on Pike Hill? This ain’t your concern, sunshine. Run on back to Rebel and stay out of it.”

“Oh Lord,” said Mrs. Mabel.

“I won’t let you get away with this,” said Minnie. “You know this is wrong. Is she even eighteen yet?”

“You have it wrong,” Serena interrupted, mortified.

“I beg your pardon?” said Minnie.

"It's not what you think at all. I appreciate your concern, Ma'am, but there's no need for all of that. I'm happy living with Roman. I'm not a child. I know what I'm doing."

"Time to go," Roman snapped, and all but dragged Serena to the checkout line.

Minnie hurried after them and caught Serena's arm. She spoke quickly, aware that Roman was rising towards an explosion. "What was your name, honey?"

"Serena."

A small white card appeared in Minnie's hand and she pressed it into Serena's tote bag. "You have options," said Minnie firmly. "If you need anything, then come to me. I'll do anything I can to help. "

"Well," said Serena as she watched Roman load groceries into the truck.

"Well, what?"

"Who was that woman?"

"My brother's fiance. Apparently."

"You don't like her."

"No."

"Why not?"

"She's interfering."

"Oh." Serena turned over the card. "She's a veterinarian. I didn't know there was a black lady vet in town." *Maybe Isaiah can be a vet someday.*

"I guess she wants a medal for it," Roman snarled.

His reaction surprised her. The woman seemed harmless enough. Maybe a little interfering, but perhaps Roman's problem had more to do with the fact that Miss Minnie Brown clearly believed he was dangerous.

"How come you never talk about your brothers?" said Serena, deciding right then to get to the bottom of it.

"What's there to say?" Roman finished loading the groceries. He opened her passenger door like he always did. "Get in."

She stayed right where she was. "I want to know why you and that lady don't get along. Why won't you just tell me? You got something to hide?"

"No," he said, the tips of his ears turning red.

"Did you sleep with her?" she said, her voice rising slightly.

"Get in the damned truck, Serena."

"Don't cuss at me. I knew it! You and that woman got a history."

"No, the fuck we don't."

"You take me for a fool — think that because I'm young I don't know nothing? Why are you lying?" She felt sick.

You are a fool! You thought this was a real relationship. How naïve can you be?

"I didn't tell you because it's ancient history that don't matter anymore."

"So what if I asked her?"

"I don't want you talking to her."

"Well now. Isn't that funny?" She wanted to hit him.

"Don't tell me you fell for her sorry act. She's like the rest of them. They just want food for gossip."

"Maybe I should find that out for myself."

"You don't need these people, Serena, damn it."

"I need to know why you don't want me talking to that woman, Roman! The real reason."

"Christ, girl." Pale with fury, he slammed the door so hard the truck rocked. "I said it's in the past. I said leave it alone. Did I get after you about the whole of Snatch Hill passing you around?"

Silence landed hard between them.

"You bastard," Serena choked. "That ain't the same thing at all. I can't believe you would say that to me."

His temper vanished as soon as it had come. He blinked. "Fuck. Serena, I didn't mean that."

"Then why did you say it?" She shouldered past him roughly. "Go to hell."

The car ride back home was tense and ugly. His words kept playing in her head. It was one of the worst things Roman could have said to her. She felt gutted and betrayed. At least he had the decency to look ashamed of himself.

"Serena, I got a damned nasty temper," he said quietly. "The truth of it is I used to have feelings for Minnie, and I didn't act like a gentleman about it."

She felt cold to her bones. "Did you rape her?"

"Jesus Christ. No–we just kissed. It's all over with. As you can tell, it ain't rainbows between us and I guess I can't blame her for that."

More silence.

"You think I'm dirty," Serena said, stating a fact.

"No. No, sugar, I don't." He reached across the console and touched her knee. His brow furrowed.

"It's alright," she said. She didn't feel like talking so she stared out the window. The days were getting colder and shorter. Her time with Roman was nearly halfway up.

"My Ma had an experience like yours," said Roman.

Serena turned. "What?"

"My Ma." He gripped the wheel with one hand so the other could pick at his jeans. Serena recognized the nervous habit. "I was born in a shack in the back hills. No lights nor water, like where I found you and Isaiah. It was hell. We'd see Pa's truck coming up the hill. Ma would send me off into the woods and tell me not to come back until sundown. One day I stayed back, and I saw what he was doing to her. My Ma was lame in one leg. She couldn't do much but beg him to stop. I wasn't big and tough back then. Just a kid, and half-starved at that." They were almost to the house. Roman's voice remained the same flat monotone. "When I was eight, Ma took sick and died.

Some kind of infection that was goin' around the back hills. When Pa showed up, he made me dig her grave before he took me away. Few years ago I went back for whatever was left. She's under the tree on my hill. The one with the bottles."

"Roman..."

He seemed to want to say more. His thumb went back and forth over the hole in his jeans, but then he apparently thought better of it and changed the subject with a blunt apology. "I was out of line, Serena. I should never have said that to you. I'm sorry."

They parked behind Mrs. Loving's car but Roman made no move to get out of the Pegasus. A bee landed on the windshield and crawled through the faint streaks of pollen.

"I won't ever talk to you like that again," he said.

Passing you around.

She was not sure if she believed him. After all, every bad man in her life had made promises like that before.

Back at the house Roman was polite to her. She watched him carefully to see if he treated Isaiah any different. He didn't. She unpacked the groceries and planned the weekly meals. She listened with half an ear as Roman explained to Isaiah how to noodle a catfish. Isaiah showed Roman his drawings. Isaiah had become chattier these last few weeks. On Pike Hill he barely talked above a whisper, now he pattered on about everything.

Roman laughed at something Isaiah said. He had a nice laugh. She liked the way he spoke to Isaiah. No babying, just straight talk. He was always kind to the boy, in fact. He called Isaiah his kin, and treated him like it. That counted for a lot.

But Serena cast an eye toward Katie McCall's bedroom, and her uncertainty returned.

There was a lot she didn't know about Roman. But today had been a lesson. She'd seen his dark side. She really hoped she never would again.

CHAPTER 11
THE LETTER

The next day the gardener handed Serena a folded note. "Came from some lady, be from your side." He spat. "What it say, then?"

"Let me read it and I'll tell you," said Serena. She opened the lined paper and read the spidery handwriting. A look of total surprise crossed her face.

"Albert, can I get a ride down the hill?" she asked the gardener.

"You surely can. I was gonna offer it, anyway."

His rush to agree surprised Serena, because she had always thought the man didn't like her. And she herself avoided him. In fact, she didn't know why Roman kept the man on at all. He was a lazy drunk. He might be a little drunk right now. It didn't feel right, Albert helping her, but she warned herself not to be paranoid. Sometimes being cooped up in a house too long made you look for danger under every flower pot.

They rumbled off the hill together. Serena hoped she could take care of this before Roman got home. Mrs. Loving had Isaiah until five, so it was really Roman finding her gone that worried her. He'd made it plain he didn't like the idea of her running off by herself. But she felt rebellious. So what if he didn't like it? Curley had done the same thing, preventing her from leaving Pike Hill. Was she Roman's prisoner? No. She didn't need freedom papers to leave the damn hill. And this little outing had nothing to do with him, anyway. Not his business. He wasn't the only one allowed to have secrets.

The meeting went poorly. Roman had prepared to talk about the next phase of the harvest– curing the marijuana in the long sheds–and his plans to inoculate a certain percentage of the bud to test for quality. Additionally, he intended to upgrade a couple more trucks for the Western route, and redirect the wastewater of certain field operations in the future. It was too bad that the important heads of the family found the subject of his beef with Curley a more pressing concern.

Adding to his annoyance was Ross, who wasn't even supposed to be there. He'd come up to deliver the papers for Serena and had tagged along. Ross didn't exactly boost confidence in the seasoned mountain men, since he obviously hadn't touched so much as a fishing pole in years, and insisted on making uncalled for quips that amused only himself.

"Challenging Curley right before the harvest is a fool move," growled Elias McCall, who was married to a Snatch Hill woman–his second cousin. "The Snatch Hills won't stand for it, Roman."

After this harvest, the Snatch Hills were going to get a hard lesson about what they could or couldn't stand.

"Is Curley sending you here to talk me out of kicking his ass?"

"We all know you could lick Curley," rumbled Hogs Green Tree, rubbing his massive belly. "That ain't the point in question. We have a mess of goddamned dope to move in three weeks' time, and I don't want Curley or his goons doing any monkey business with my harvest."

"It's the family's harvest," Roman reminded him. *And I hold the land in title, old man.*

Hogs glared. "Return the little witch like he's asking for. Settle things down."

"No," said Roman.

The uncles exchanged looks. Elias's red mustache quivered. Of the two, he had the worse temper. Looking at Uncle Elias was like looking at Duke McCall if Roman's father was cursed with red hair and poor nutrition. The man's green eyes always watered as if he was about to sneeze. "I suspect, boy," said Elias in tones of a man finally about to have his say, "That this is all a scheme you and Rebel have cooked up together. You're planning something with the darkies. I'm liable to think this scheme goes deeper than most of us realize. You're in cahoots with Black Florin, Roman. Admit it!"

Ross badly concealed a snort. Elias reddened. "Did I say something amusing, boy?"

"Not at all." Ross drawled, his Charleston accent dripping with condescension. "I merely seemed to have got a little pepper up my nose."

"You think it's funny? This ain't some urban liberal hell-hole," Elias snarled. "This is our home. We had our suspicions about you, gypsy. But for Duke's sake we stayed quiet. He ain't cold in the grave, but you and your brothers are hellbent on destroying everything he built. We like Florin the way it is. Separate. Keep them off our side."

"My issue with Curley has nothing to do with that."

"Really? Because to me, it shows where your loyalties lie. With them."

"By protecting a woman from Curley McCall, I'm letting Black Florin pull you from your bed at night and line you up against a barn? That's quite the theory, Uncle Elias."

"Don't play the fool, Roman. We've always known where your priorities lie," Hogs put in recklessly, backing up his friend. Elias gave him a warning look, but the Green Tree man blundered on, "We know your own mother was one of 'em. Yes, I know Duke wanted it hushed, but Duke's dead now, ain't he? Murdered in cold blood. And I've heard rumors it was a nigger that killed him. Ain't that interesting. Fishy. Duke gets a bullet in the dark, and now suddenly the halfbreed's running the show."

"The what?" said Ross.

Roman's eyes glittered with annoyance. He ignored the remark about his race. He was there to listen.

"You haven't found his killer yet. Maybe because you ain't trying to find him. Maybe because you was in on it," Hogs finished in a huff.

Ross shifted. Roman pressed his foot under the table. "The fact is, Duke is dead," said Roman. "And you have to deal with me. I was Duke's right hand, and bastard or not, I kept this family fed while Duke played dress-up with you boys. I'm ready to hand you a payload from this harvest, gentlemen. All I ask is you stay out of my private affairs."

"Your affairs are the clan affairs."

"No, Uncle Hogs. My affairs are nobody's motherfucking business, actually."

Hogs opened his mouth and Roman interrupted calmly, "Do we have a problem here, boys?"

That shut them up. Both men turned red. The hard country challenge was undeniable. It meant Roman was prepared to resolve this matter right here and now in a far less diplomatic fashion. Bad-tempered Hogs looked game, but luckily Elias' cowardice spared him.

"If I believe you're turning the family down the wrong path, I won't sit quiet," Elias growled, scraping back from the table to save face by having the last word. "Let's go, Hogs. We made our point."

In the parking lot Roman smoked, his thick fingers crushing the end of the cigarette until it nearly bent in half. His face was still; an iron mask.

"Did you let word slip about Pa's killer?" He asked Ross.

"No. I didn't tell anybody." Ross frowned. "Why did they call you a halfbreed, Roman?"

"Because my Ma was Black." It was almost a relief to just say it. Why not? It was the truth.

"I never knew." Ross rubbed his jaw. "Really?"

"Yeah."

"I thought you looked kind of like that woman. Julette. Roman, she isn't your *grandmother*?"

"It would seem so."

"Christ." Ross eyed him, waiting for him to elaborate. He didn't. Finally, Ross got the message and went to his car. He took a manila folder from his briefcase and handed it to his older brother. "Here are your girl's documents, as you requested."

Cigarette clamped between his teeth, Roman flipped through the papers with his thumb. The envelope contained Serena's paper record. Birth certificates and social security cards for her and Isaiah, medical history... everything he'd asked for. Ross's connections ran deep in Rowanville, and he was a terrier for digging up information. Roman passed Ross a thick stack of folded bills.

"I don't need that," Ross said.

"Take it."

"Save it for Rain's bail money."

Roman snorted, though it wasn't really funny. "Look, I appreciate it, Ross. Really."

"Hmph." Ross stared out at the view with him. "How is the girl?"

"She's fine."

"You really care for her. I'll be damned."

Roman didn't reply. Why did everybody think he was just some machine who couldn't love or feel? Only Serena seemed to understand that he was just a little rough around the edges. She never made assumptions about him, or judged.

And I was a dick to her.

Ross lit a cigarette with his fancy silver lighter. It was the one thing he'd taken with him from the mountain– his love of trashy cigarettes. Roman wouldn't touch a Marlboro if his life depended on it. He preferred Newports. The brothers smoked in silence.

Roman gazed out at the rolling green pasture that bordered Mayberry land. He wondered just how much of Florin Serena had actually seen. He ought to take her around more. Isaiah needed friends his age–boys. Roman would have to look into getting the boy a place at the Baptist school in town, but then again, only children from White Florin went there. It needed some thought. Roman had a lot of ideas for Isaiah's future, and some he'd shared with Serena, others, he hadn't. Because at the core of every idea, like a hard pit in a cherry, was the implication that he wanted her to stay. With him. In a forever kind of way.

Roman had reached some hard realizations about himself and Serena. He would never let her go. Ever. He wanted Serena, and if it cost him the whole fucking family, so be it.

“What will you do about Elias?” Ross asked, pulling him back to the present.

“Let him huff and puff. It’s Curley I’m worried about.”

“You’ll take care of him.”

“Yes,” Roman agreed. “Trouble is, the little bastard won’t ever leave Snatch Hill. When he does, he’s got his bodyguards. Tracking him down would be easier if I had time.”

If I wasn’t running back home every minute to be with Serena.

“I don’t want any witnesses, so that rules out busting his ass in broad daylight. I’m paranoid enough we’re gonna bring the damn Feds up here with all this carryin’-on Rebel did. Our Pa did something right in keeping everything up here in house.”

“That’s the trouble with this age we’re in,” said Ross, raising an eyebrow in the way all the McCall brothers did. “Too many paper trails.”

Ross was right. There would be no way to keep a big story from leaving these hills. Little fires. He could manage little fires. But what if this situation with Duke’s murder and the schism with Curley blazed out of control?

It was hard for Roman to know who to trust these days. Everybody felt jittery about Duke getting killed. Suspicions and rumors whirled. Roman heard them everywhere, even down in Rowanville: Duke McCall, the bedrock of the mountain, was dead and his menacing gypsy son had begun a reign of tyranny.

Handle him clean. Handle him quiet. Like always.

But that cloak-and-dagger business had its own risks. He listened to the talk. This thing with Curley was dividing opinions. Many people were simmering for a revolt. So even if Curley was to drop dead of pneumonia tomorrow, everybody would say Roman had spit in his dip can and infected him on purpose.

"You could always come work for me," offered Ross. "Rowanville isn't so bad."

Roman burst out laughing before he realized Ross was serious. Ross glared at him, exasperated but amused. "I wasn't joking."

"I know. Sorry. But I ain't leaving Florin, Ross. This is my place. It's what I was bred for, the same way you was bred for cotillions and patent leather shoes."

Ross rolled his eyes. "There's a lot to be said for holding political power, Roman. You can actually make a positive change without breaking the law."

"You think kissing ass in ballrooms is gonna get me anywhere? This place can run itself with the right leadership. It just needs the right leadership."

"Violence is like a disease. Once this mountain's infected, you won't be able to stop it from spreading. Just get out while you can. Then you don't have to worry about that girl getting her throat cut over a bullshit turf war you don't even really care about."

"I'm handling it, Ross."

"Well, the offer stands."

Roman shook his head. Florin and Serena were his blood. *I won't choose. I'll have both, or none.*

Roman drove home slowly. His thumb tapped on the wheel. He was going back home to Serena. He wanted her like an ache deep in his bones.

He couldn't wait to see her again. *She was so sweet. Sweeter than I ever imagined.* He pictured Serena lying down, legs dangling off the edge of his bed. Kneeling before her exposed pussy and separating her dark labia, which was sticky with his pale seed. Tears ran down her face, beading on her lashes. Puffy, bruised, bitten lips. He fingered her until she came all over his hands, and he licked the trail of her off his wrist and went right back to taste it from the source.

I can't believe you would say that to me.

Roman bit his tongue, angry. He gripped his hard dick through his jeans, squeezing the thick member roughly as if to punish himself. He didn't deserve to ever have her again after his blowup over Minnie fucking Brown. *Dumb bastard–dumb caveman son of a bitch–you blew it.*

The look in Serena's eyes devastated him. But he'd make it up to her. He'd get her anything she wanted–something frivolous and feminine and impractical and vastly over-priced. He'd take her and Isaiah out. And then maybe just the two of them. He'd spend big on a weekend somewhere, just him and Serena, a place where she could wear some-thing pretty that he would take his time peeling off her. A steak-and-champagne kind of place... and he could fuck her all night long in a strange bed, or under the stars...

Laughing with her, holding her, watching that stupid Preacher Man show for hours tangled up in a bed.

When Roman blew past the Greasy Hog, for a moment he thought his depraved fantasy had caused him to hallucinate. He slammed down so hard on the brakes the truck nearly spun off-road. The stench of burning rubber choked him; the image of Serena in the window was replaced by a bloodred mist. No. He was seeing things. That wasn't her...

Just Curley's truck, parked outside.

It was her.

Roman slammed open his glove box and palmed his Glock. He left his truck in the middle of the road and blazed into the honky-tonk.

A dozen pairs of startled eyes jumped to the door. The usual seedy crowd. Some McCalls, some others from the Back Hills.

"Where is she?" he asked quietly.

Someone pointed. People scattered as he stalked towards the stairs. "Jesus God, Roman, don't! Don't do it!" Begged Simms, the owner, extracting himself from the lap of a heavyset blonde. "Don't kill the fella in here. Kill him outside! Outside!"

What sounded like a scream came from the end of the upstairs hall. A scream of pain, or pleasure? It definitely belonged to Serena. Roman pounded towards the sound. He rapped sharply on the door.

"Who is it?" snarled Curley, sounding like a lover annoyed to be interrupted pleasuring his woman. Roman slammed his boot into the door and it exploded off its hinges in a shower of termite dust.

"Jesus God!" Wailed Simms. "Don't tear up the place ! Kill him outside!"

The dirty room took shape before Roman's eyes. He saw a bare mattress and a table, a greasy lamp, and Curley's jacket hanging on a chair. The man himself leapt up from the bed. His eyes widened in fear. Roman racked the slide on his gun, but fast as a weasel Curley jumped through the open window and landed in the bushes below with a crash. Roman, already leaping to the window, scrambled to get a bead on him. Curley scrambled faster, skirting the edge of the building to rush to his truck.

BLAM.

Missed. Just as Roman raised the gun again, ready to separate Curley's kneecap from its socket, Serena took a running leap at his arm and clamped on it with all her strength.

The shot went wide. Staggering back, Roman righted himself on the bedpost. It was then he noticed where Serena's clothes had gone. He lurched back to the window and emptied the clip after Curley, who was peeling out of the lot. Bullets punched through the Hurricane's sides, a window exploded, but once rubber met the road, the Hurricane was off like lightning. Dust and gravel sprayed into the air.

Roman re-holstered his empty Glock and turned on Serena.

She shrank against the bed, her beautiful eyes huge in her small face. She wore only her bra and panties. He could see no visible bruises on her skin, which meant she'd gone to

Curley willingly. Red mist. The hand holding the gun shook. He needed to calm down, or he'd shoot them both right now in this dirty whorehouse.

Roman snatched up the dress from the bedpost and thrust it at her.

"Let's go."

"Hold on," she stammered, trying to shrug back into the dress. "I can explain."

"Oh no," he said coldly, jerking her hands down as she tried to cover herself. "As you were, sweetheart."

"Roman — please—"

So be it. He took away the dress. "Outside. Now."

She stopped only to grab something green and fuzzy off the nightstand. Roman recognized the item but had no time to stop and wonder what Serena was doing with Isaiah's stuffed dinosaur in the middle of a rendezvous with Curley. Serena hurried past the shattered door, her face drawn and terrified. In the hall, the stench of sex was like a physical object.

Down the hall, a door cracked open on a potbellied roughneck sitting on a dirty mattress, knees spread while a naked woman sloppily sucked his dick. It was like they hadn't heard Roman shooting up the place through less than a foot of drywall. The woman moaned, slipping the roughneck's stubby cock from her mouth. The man stood up, muttering filth as he jerked off in her face. Ropes of semen splatted across the woman's fleshy tits; she moaned like a good little whore.

For a small fee, the Greasy Hog allowed women to use these back rooms to sell their wares. To find Serena in a place like this...

His hand tightened viciously on her arm. "Is that what you want, Serena?" He said in her ear, not recognizing his voice. He shook her. "You want that? To get your holes fucked in a dirty back room?"

"You got it all wrong," she whispered desperately, squeezing Isaiah's Dinosaur to her chest. "Let me get dressed. I can explain..."

"Shut the fuck up."

He marched her half-naked past the whispering crowd gathered in the Greasy Hog taproom.

Somebody had moved Roman's truck to the shoulder. His cousin Eliza Jane leaned against the truckbed, sucking on a Marls Red. She wordlessly handed Roman the keys.

After thanking her, Roman opened the passenger door and levered Serena inside. He slammed the door on her protest.

He turned to his cousin. "Did you see what happened?"

Eliza pushed out her lower lip. "Curley went inside with your girl and asked Simms for a room. She came with 'im in his truck."

"Willingly?" He bit out.

"Far as I could tell."

That was all he needed to know. Roman asked about her children and barely listened to her reply. Eliza Jane slunk off, and he walked on heavy feet to his driver's side.

Serena had dressed. She wiped her eyes when he got in.

"Roman —"

"You're off my hill. You leave tonight."

"Roman! Listen to me," She cried. "You have it wrong. It's not how it looks at all."

He started the truck.

"Roman, they have Isaiah. That's what Curley said. L-look. I got this note today..." She patted in the pocket of her dress. Her face sank. "Shoot! It must have fallen out in the room."

He could barely see the road. "Stop talking."

"It's true. Curley tricked me into going to Green Hill. He s-said they had Mrs. Loving and Isaiah. He showed me this— " She waved the stuffed Dinosaur at him. Roman had no idea what to make of that, but it infuriated him that she would use her son to cover up her deceit.

"Mrs. Loving and Isaiah were gone all morning — I believed Curley when he said his boys had trapped them. Curley said if I s-slept with him he'd let Isaiah go..." Her voice cracked. The sound was more unbearable than her stammered lies.

Slow down.

He eased his foot off the gas. He could barely breathe. "Lying... little cunt. You little... After everything... I did for you."

Her eyes widened in horror. She looked terrified and wretched–he didn't blame her. He was going to explode.

"Roman! Believe me," she begged. Roman's cellphone vibrated in his pocket. He dragged the device out. "Some luck," he snarled, tossing it in Serena's lap. The screen read MRS. LOVING.

"Answer it," he ordered. "On speaker."

Serena scrambled to do so. "Mrs. Loving? Is Isaiah with you? Are you okay? Oh God, is he alright?"

Her commitment to the lie was impressive. Roman thought dazedly that he'd never been more wrong about a woman.

"Serena! Honey! We're just fine. Are you alright?" Came Mrs. Loving's sugar-pie voice. "What's the matter?"

"I'm f-fine. Is Isaiah there? Can I talk to him?"

"No," snarled Roman, snatching the phone from her. He couldn't bear to hear the little boy's voice. He'd been so blind to everything.

"Serena seems to think the Snatch Hills kidnapped you," Roman said to Mrs. Loving. "Yet you seem to be in good feather. Did somebody pay your ransom?"

"Kidnapped?" Mrs. Loving exclaimed, surprised at his sarcasm. "They could wish it! Didn't you read my message?"

"Mrs. Loving—" Serena attempted to break in. Roman gave her a murderous look, and she fell silent. Oblivious, Mrs. Loving went on. "Kidnapped? No, Roman, nobody kidnapped me, but I tell you these Snatch Hills sure tried it today."

"What do you mean?"

"Well, Isaiah and I were at the Queen's General Store— and I don't want to hear it, Roman. Their prices are lower than McCall's General and that's a fact. Some of Curley's kin — don't know their names — pinned us in like a band of jackals."

"Oh my God," said Serena, slumping in the seat.

"Yes, honey," said Mrs. Loving. "I put Isaiah down, and then I laid those hooligans out with the pepper spray. And then I took my purse and laid them out again. The old Queensbury saw the commotion and drove 'em off. What was that, Isaiah? Here, talk to your Mama now."

"Ma?" Isaiah yelled into the phone. "Ma, I lost Dinosaur!"

Serena put a shaking hand over her mouth and closed her eyes. But her voice was steady. "I have him, baby. Dinosaur is safe and sound."

"Really?" Isaiah said. "How?"

"He came to find us when he got separated from you. Now he's going to get coffee with me and Mister Roman."

"Dinosaur doesn't like coffee. He likes apple juice," Isaiah chided.

"Are you alright, Isaiah?" Serena said, giving up the game.

"Yes, I'm fine," the child said. "Mrs. Loving hit the man with the purse. It was funny."

Mrs. Loving took the phone again. "Will you and Roman be awhile on your errand, dearie? Isaiah and I are driving home now."

Roman spoke loudly over Serena. “Did anybody deliver a note today, Mrs. Loving? For Serena?”

“A note? No, I didn’t see a note.”

Roman scowled. “Alright. We’ll be home soon.”

“I’ll check for a note when I get to the house, honey. Goodbye!”

“Curley must have got the toy from his cousins,” Serena said dully, working the mystery out as the road blurred through the windows. “It fell when Mrs. Loving got jumped. Oh, he had me convinced.” She rocked back in the seat, looking sick. “He picked me up on Pike Hill, Roman. I’d gone to see my Uncle Ray. I thought... I got that note saying Uncle Ray was sick. Curley set me up.”

“You didn’t recognize your Uncle’s handwriting?” *She’s lying. She’s got Mrs. L wrapped around her finger...covering up for her.*

“Uncle Ray can’t read or write. He gets people to do it for him all the time,” Serena explained. “Curley had Isaiah’s Dinosaur...” She held the stuffed animal out. “He was saying all these things... Saying how he would k-kill Isaiah. All he wanted was sex. I didn’t know what to do. I went with him.”

“You didn’t think to call me — you didn’t think—”

“I don’t have a phone, Roman,” Serena whispered.

It was true. Serena had mentioned going to Rowanville to set herself up with a device, but other errands got in the way. She barely left the house, so what was the hurry?

Roman rubbed his jaw. “Alright. Go on.”

"When we got upstairs at the bar, I knew I couldn't do it. I couldn't let him do that to me again. I thought I could try to grab his gun—"

"A stupid idea. He would have shot you."

"I didn't care. He was talking so crazy. I thought he might be on some drugs. I started moving to the window, thinking I could at least try to jump out." She put a hand to her cheek, staring glassily out the windshield. "I was just so scared. If you hadn't come in, I don't know what would have happened. Imagine me thinking they had Isaiah... Not knowing what they would do to him if I didn't let Curley... Let him..." She covered her face.

Roman clung desperately to the last embers of his fury. But it was no use. He pulled off down an abandoned holler, tires sinking into deeply treaded ruts. He switched to four-wheel drive. They bounced down the track until they met the edge of the North River. Roman turned the keys. Silence. Birdsong.

He rubbed his face. He didn't know what to think. He hated seeing Serena cry.

"Curley must have got the Dinosaur from the parking lot. It was the only reason I went with him. Isaiah never lets that toy out of his sight."

Roman said huskily, "Just an hour ago I let it be known I wasn't giving you up to Curley. Now a host of people just saw you go willingly into the Greasy Hog with him. Into a whore-room. How the fuck do you think this looks, Serena?"

She wiped her eyes. “You should have let me put my dress on.”

“I thought you’d fucked Curley.” His chest heaved. “Did you?”

“No. I swear, Roman.”

“You’re damned lucky I was driving by.”

She hung her head. “I know.”

His callused hands clenched and unclenched the steering wheel.

“Thank you,” she said.

He scowled at the tranquil scene before him. The North River had some of his favorite fishing spots. He knew another spot where the fishing wasn’t so nice. But with a towel, a cooler, and a pretty woman down for anything, a man might have himself an exciting afternoon.

Of course, they weren’t here for that.

“Now I really have to kill the son of a bitch,” he said.

“Don’t kill Curley, Roman.”

Because you want to fuck him? He was going to lose it.

He got out of the truck. No cigarettes. No nothing. If only he could rip something apart with his bare hands. Boiling blood pumped hard through his veins.

Serena came round the side of the truck. “Roman?”

Roman grabbed her wrist, feeling her delicate bones slide between his hard fingers. Her skin was the softest thing he’d ever felt. *I could hurt her without even trying.*

“Curley is a dead man,” he told her. He closely watched her reaction.

Serena’s lips turned down at the corners. “You think I’m asking you not to kill him for myself? It’s your soul I’m worried for.”

“I’ve killed men before.”

“He’s your cousin.”

“I’ve killed cousins before. This ain’t new to me. You don’t want him dead? Surprising, after all he’s done to you.”

“I just couldn’t watch you do it,” Serena whispered. “Yeah, I want him dead. World would be better off without a man like Curley. But I couldn’t watch you do it.”

“Why, damn it?”

“Killing, killing, killing. Won’t be any room for love. And Roman, I l-love you.” She brushed away a tear. “I just want it to stop. I want to have you without all this ugliness. Are you angry with me?”

“No.” He cupped her waist. “Get in the car.”

“Where are we going?”

“Home.”'

While Serena put Isaiah to bed, Roman ferreted out the gardener, Albert.

“Did you deliver a note to Serena?” He asked.

“No, sir,” said Albert.

"Let's try that again. Did you deliver a note to Serena, motherfucker?"

Albert flinched. "Uh, yes, sir," he sniffed. He reeked of whiskey.

"Who gave it to you?"

"Don't remember."

Roman gripped him by the scruff. "Really? Give it some thought."

"Ow! It was one of Curley's boys," Albert cringed. "He told me to make sure she got it. Said Curley jes' wanted to talk..."

"You set her up."

"Curley told me I could have the pills," Albert whined.

"What pills?"

"His blue pills." Albert whimpered as Roman clamped on the back of his neck. Pinpoint pupils danced madly in the gardener's eyes.

"You high right now?" Roman growled.

"I ain't no junkie," Albert protested. "It's just these blue pills from the city. Curley gave me a couple— I use 'em for my back — ARGH!"

"You got an hour. I want you off my hill," Roman told the quivering heap at his feet. "Or your back won't be the only thing needing Curley's pills."

Albert staggered to his knees. "No... please."

"Be glad I didn't just shoot you."

"I worked years for you," the man said. "Worked hard. I was loyal. Now you let that nigger girl sit pretty in your house like a queen, gettin' paid..."

But Roman was immovable. In an hour's time Albert had his Chevy full of his worldly possessions, including a dozen empty bottles of hooch that must have had some sentimental value which Roman couldn't fathom.

Roman had known Albert was a drunk who never let a dollar get comfortable in his pocket. He'd tolerated the gardener's shortcomings, judging him a harmless fool who could still grow some damned good tomatoes when all was said and done. But this thing with Serena stunned him. He'd trusted the man around his daughter. But now he knew the man would hand over an innocent young woman to Curley without compunction.

You let that nigger girl sit like a queen in your house...

And there it was. Had Serena been just another yellow-haired bird he plucked out of some bullshit holler, nobody would care. That she had dark skin and came from the wrong side of Florin had everybody running around with their hands on their asses.

Too bad.

He felt invigorated by the realization that he didn't give a fuck anymore. He'd spent his life living by the mountain's rules. Now it was time the mountain lived by Roman's rules.

Once Albert was gone, Roman locked the now-vacant cabin, which a glance told him he would have to gut and clean completely. His nose burned at the stench of old beer and stale tobacco spit. Too much garbage taking up space in his life, trying to crush the one good thing he had.

Time to clean house.

Roman walked to the guest house and quietly let himself inside. He took off his boots and laid out on Serena's couch without making a sound. Serena was just putting the boy down to bed. Roman heard murmurs and quiet laughter coming from Isaiah's room. The sound of running water moved through the walls like static, and her voice rose and fell like a slow wave on a riverside beach. The pounding in his head eased.

Finally he heard Serena shut Isaiah's door and go to her own room down the hall. Roman followed her.

He picked up a book on the nightstand titled TAKING THE GED- WHAT YOU NEED TO KNOW. A workbook sat neatly next to it. Roman studied her handwriting under the bedside lamp. The letters were big and girly, but very uniform. She had filled damn near every page already. He knew she stayed up late every night to catch up on what she'd missed from school. He saw library books stacked against the other wall of the room, books on whatever Florin's meager little library could get its hands on. She was trying desperately to catch up on lost time.

Roman recognized and respected grit. He loved that about her. He knew he could never underestimate Serena. She was sweet, but had a fire for life inside her.

The water shut off and Serena came back to the room with her towel in hand. She jumped when she saw him. "Oh! Roman?"

She wasn't panicked, or crying, or throwing vases at his head. She looked relieved.

She wants me.

"You're wearing one of them nighties," he said appreciatively.

"It's my favorite from what you got me." She spun in a small circle, showing off the yellow lace getup, which cut away in the middle to reveal her smooth brown stomach. "You like it?"

"Hell yeah." He rested back on the bed, taking her in. "You got any more?"

She threw the towel at him. "Too bad you stopped our little deal before I could wear the rest for you."

"The deal is back on."

"Good. How did you get in here?"

"Through the front door."

She shook a finger at him. "I knew it. You could unlock it the whole time."

"I wanted to see you. I couldn't wait all night."

She hesitated. "So you're not still mad?"

"No. I'm here to say sorry. Again."

Her face lost expression. The lingerie was a soft, butter-colored yellow that intensified the dark tone of her skin.

She sat next to him on the edge of the bed and began braiding up her hair, her eyes faraway.

"How is he?" Roman asked.

"Isaiah's sleeping," she said. "With Dinosaur at the foot of the bed."

"All's right with the world," Roman rumbled. He took her hand. "Hey."

"It's all good, Roman."

"I should have trusted you."

She said quietly, "I know. But in fairness, I used the note as an excuse to leave the hill and rattle you for not knowing where I was. I was being spiteful on purpose. Maybe I got what was coming."

He said, "I don't believe that. I should have known you'd never go to Curley. I just thought you'd... left." *Everybody leaves.*

"Roman, I'd never in a million years leave you for Curley McCall."

"I just keep replaying it in my head. When I saw you in there. I just saw what my own sick head wanted to see, and I didn't even think."

"I think it scared you, what you saw in that room. But you didn't want to be scared, so you just got angry," Serena said thoughtfully. "Anger can be stronger than fear, but it's like a fire that hardly knows what it's burning."

Well said. Roman rubbed the back of her hand with his thumb. "If you could have anything in the world right now, what would it be?"

She took her hand away to finish the other braid. "Steak and lobster."

He grinned. "Something that ain't food."

"An elephant."

"An *elephant*?"

"Just to ride one. I don't think I can feed an elephant even with a kitchen like yours."

"You say the damndest things." Some of her hair oil got on his fingers. Nutmeg and coconut. Tropical. He imagined Serena on a beach in a bikini, sun kissing her dark brown skin. He'd rub oil on her head to toe and make love to her in a hammock or some other exotic type of a bed.

"I can't remember the last time I left the mountain on a pleasure trip," he admitted.

"You didn't go nowhere with your daughter?"

He shook his head. "I was always too busy or we were fighting over bullshit. "

"That's a shame," she said.

It was.

"Where would you go with Isaiah?" he asked.

Serena stretched out on the bed. "I don't know. I want to go everywhere. There's still so much to see." She grinned. "And once I have my yacht..."

He smacked her ass, and she rolled on top of him, bearing him down into the bed. I forgive you, her eyes said.

He pushed at her chin with his thumb. "I mean it. Where would you go if you could go anywhere?"

"New Orleans," she replied. "Always wanted to see it, eat the food."

"Of course," he teased.

"Hush! I mean it. But I guess it ain't really a place for kids, and I'd want to take Isaiah. Maybe we can go to a good museum. With dinosaurs. You know how he likes those." She pushed her mouth to one side. "But after that, I should say Rome. Or Morocco. I saw it in a book one time. It looked nice." She smiled. "You kind of look Moroccan. Not like I ever met a Moroccan to know."

"I can promise you I'm not Moroccan."

She met his eyes. "What are you, then?"

"I don't know. Some freak of nature."

"I don't think that."

"Well, thanks I guess." He felt relaxed and calm. Serena had no judgment for him, no bitter words. He held out his arm against hers, his gold skin against her brown. "I don't know. What am I?"

"Hairy," she joked. She ran a hand up under his shirt, her palms pressing on his bare skin.

"You happy?"

"Right now? Yeah, I am." She rested her head on his chest. "You always ask me that."

Roman said roughly, "I'd like to make you happy all the time, sugar."

"Nobody's happy all the time, Mister Roman." She sighed and buried her face in his arm. "Mm," she said. "You always smell like... I don't know. I don't even know."

He tucked her closer against his body, staring up at the rafters. Her heartbeat slowed. He stroked her soft skin and hair. He loved this. Just doing this. Why did he ever have to stop?

Roman woke up from a nightmare with his dick hard and his heart raging in his chest. He clutched blindly at the sweat-soaked sheets, for a crazed instant thinking he was still falling down a black hole in the ground.

"Roman?" Serena's softness curled against him. "What's wrong?"

He swallowed hard to calm his racing heart. *Awake. Alive.*

"Roman?"

"Nothin'. Go back to sleep."

"You scared the hell out of me. You sure you okay?"

"I'm fine." He put her back in the same position, with her head on his chest. He was sweating a little, but she didn't mind.

Her hand moved lower and cupped him. Her husky sleep-drugged voice said, "You need something? To forget it?"

His dick was hard, because in the dream he'd been afraid. So afraid. But now he wasn't afraid. Now he was furious, jittery, exhausted, and hard. His cock pulsed against her grip, hot and painful.

No. Better just go to sleep.

She palmed him, squeezing up on his cockhead.

"Let me make you forget it. Just be here with me." She swung a leg over his hips, straddling him, stroking his chest.

I love this woman.

He pulled her to him. Serena's mouth opened under his and she took his aggressive kiss in stride, her soft lips offering themselves to him. He scrolled her pretty nightie down.

She made soft, desperate sounds as he sucked her big breasts. The dark, thick nipples that signified her motherhood rubbed against his tongue. Her hips twirled over his cock. He jerked his jeans and belt down, kicked them off... they clattered to the floor. Serena and Roman froze, listening, waiting. But no sound came from Isaiah's room.

He grabbed Serena gently by the throat and kissed her again, her lips fitting against his perfectly, her mouth warm and tasting like lemon and honey. The sheets twisted underneath them.

"Roman," she whispered. "I'm sorry. About Curley."

"It's alright." He prised open her legs and fisted his bare cock, pulling aside her silky lingerie with the other hand.

"You're the only man I want."

She was dry. He fucked two fingers slowly into her mouth. Her tongue darted out to spread hot saliva over his knuckles. He slowly prepared her lower down. In no time she was slippery and warm. He lined himself up.

She gasped.

"You good?"

"Don't stop."

He worked another inch inside her. She writhed on top of him. "Oh God, Roman. How is it so big?"

He fought his way through her tightness, her beautiful dark body opening to service him, the way it should always be. Her arousal frothed around his dick as he steadily pumped her.

"Every man in that bar was staring at you. Staring at your ass...at these." He pinched her nipples and she curled forward with a soft cry. "You know what they thought. They wanted to take you in one of those rooms...Bend you over and fuck you. And they wouldn't be gentle, neither."

Her nails raked down his chest. "No?" she panted.

"Naw," he hissed, hips thudding into hers. Her cunt was sticky and slick, widening to accept him but still amazingly tight. "All of 'em taking turns on you... coming inside you. I'd fuckin' kill them. I'd kill anybody that touched you."

Serena clenched around him. His rhythm broke for a moment as he struggled not to lose it. She gasped and wrapped her arms around his neck. "That's sick," she whispered.

"They could all watch me using you. Watch my seed making rivers down your legs. Because you're mine, baby-girl. You're my woman."

"You're crazy," she moaned. "Harder. You're so deep. I can feel you so deep..."

She caressed him with her insides, braving his size so she could love on him from his head to his toes. So he wouldn't feel monstrous and broken, but like a man worth loving through all the bullshit. She took a little pain to give him so much pleasure. And wouldn't he do the same for her, a thousand times?

I can protect her from everyone but me.

He gave it to her loose and dirty, being rough on purpose. She cried out, knees twitching together. He forced them apart and smudged his thumb against her most sensitive point, rising up, holding her.

When she came, he bit down savagely on her breast. Her fingers clutched handfuls of his hair. His thick curly hair that looked more like hers than any McCall's.

Was love just a man's own reflection in a woman's eyes? He pulled out of her and flipped her over in the damp sheets. When her hand scrabbled for the pillow, he trapped it under his own. He nudged her knees apart and mounted her.

Time slid away from them. He plunged again and again into Serena, and then the last barrier of restraint broke, and Roman didn't pull out. With a groan his male organs clenched and released as he pumped ropes of cum into her tight body, his life mating with hers in the deepest place there was.

Serena turned around, sliding away from him. He grunted and came again into the sheets. A splash of cream across her smooth dark thighs.

“Baby,” he murmured, cupping her chin and pressing his forehead to hers. Roman felt completely drained; as if he didn’t exist anywhere else but in this bed with Serena. “My girl...”

In dazed disbelief he ran a thumb through the creamy seed flowing out of her pussy. *His* seed.

More than enough to get her pregnant. *You crazy bastard, what have you done?*

The love in her honey gaze was no reflection, but its own fire, burning brightly from her soul. She opened her legs and tilted her hips and slid his still-hard dick inside her tight, slick, overflowing pussy. *Fuck. Fuck.* She gave him a slutty, open-mouthed kiss that had him fucking her again without thinking.

“More,” she whispered. “More. All of you... Everything.”

CHAPTER 12

ROMAN'S GAMBIT

Roman took her to Rowanville the next morning.

Serena wore a short yellow dress and sandals, with her hair up in an exploding pineapple bun that flattered her round face. She slid into Roman's truck, tucking her bag neatly in her lap.

"Good morning. Again. I think Isaiah definitely heard us last night because he asked me what time you left this morning."

"Should I talk to him?"

"Maybe you should," said Serena, looking back at the house with a smile. "He might be a little jealous."

"We won't be gone long," Roman said, his eyes traveling over her. "I'll get him something while we're in the valley. You're wearing that?"

"You like it?" She nervously tugged the hem.

She'd saved up this dress for a special occasion. Today felt like one, even if the #1 item on the to-do list was not that romantic: a trip to the drugstore to make sure their "accident" last night didn't result in a baby. Roman rubbed some of the floaty material of her dress between his big fingers. Then he turned on the ignition and said, "I didn't plan to get into a fight today."

"Is it too short?"

"Yes."

"If you really don't like it, then–"

"You'll change?"

"I was going to say too bad. I bought this from the thrift store with Mrs. Loving one time."

"Really? It's cute." He reached up and snapped her panty waistband. "But I want these."

"Oh hell no. You're not getting my panties! Roman, no!"

He slid them down her legs, the little number vanishing in his enormous grip. He stuffed the scrap of fabric into his pocket. "Thank you," he said, wearing the mischievous grin she saw more frequently these days.

"I better get those back," Serena warned.

"Uh-huh." Roman put his hand on her knee as they drove off the hill, removing it only to wave at another pickup coming in the opposite direction. "That's Sam Bailey," he told Serena. "He's watching the house while we're gone. Until I take care of Curley, I want you to have some protection. I think he's getting bolder. Going after Mrs. Loving in public? That's low even for the Snatch Hills."

"Do you trust Sam Bailey?" Serena asked.

"Reliable folks, the Baileys. I trust Sam with my life."

So it seemed like Roman would go through with his plan to kill Curley. Serena bit her lip. She hoped it didn't backfire. Why did she have such a bad feeling?

Just don't think about that now. You're going down the mountain, alone, with Roman. Almost like a date.

She touched Roman's hand on her knee, and he kept it there for the whole ride down the mountain.

Between her legs still felt wet and sore from all the cum he'd dumped inside her. She pressed her thighs together, ashamed to be aroused by what he'd done.

Well, she didn't know how to feel. It was hard enough to tell how he felt. Did he want to get her pregnant? In the moment it seemed like it. He came twice more inside her before they stopped, both shaking with exhaustion. He stroked her and whispered that he'd always take care of her and Isaiah, that he loved her. And then he opened her legs and made love to her a fourth time, getting another load deep. So deep.

But in the morning cold reality doused passions. He saw the seed still glistening in the puffy folds of her sex and he started talking rapidly, which wasn't usual for Roman. He said he didn't want to force her to have his baby. He'd been reckless and careless with her future. He blamed himself even when Serena pointed out she'd done half of the work of laying down in bed with him.

Her actions made little sense to her either, and even right now she felt strangely calm. She must have been out of her mind to sleep with a man without protection at this point in her life. Out of her mind or utterly stupid. But damn, a woman's body just betrayed her when it got underneath a man, and all her feelings for Roman came out last night and in that bed. After that horrible day, she wanted nothing but to spend all night getting dicked down by his skilled and tireless body. She liked that she could be rough as she wanted and it didn't hurt him at all. She could just be wild. Unafraid. She thought about how much she loved him, how he had protected her from the very beginning, and she couldn't shake the sense that it was just right to be with Roman in that way.

But did she want a baby?

She wanted another child, someday. Of course she did. Serena loved all children, and she wanted Isaiah to have a sibling. But every wise woman knew what a man promised in bed changed at the speed of light the minute a baby got in the mix.

No; there was nothing under the law and nobody under heaven to stop Roman putting her and Isaiah out if she got pregnant. Likely it would happen the minute he lost interest in sleeping with her.

She didn't want to believe that could happen. One half of her brain wove fantasies of a happily ever after with Roman and Isaiah. But could she gamble with Isaiah's future right now? No. He came first. Period. And until she had her own place and money in the bank, there could be no extra baby for Serena Jones. Hell, she didn't even have a bank account yet — but that would change today. Part of the reason they drove down to Rowanville was to set her up with her own cards and accounts.

But first things first

Roman made her wait in the car as he walked into the drugstore. She watched his powerful body stride towards the glass doors. He wore his "going out clothes": black T-shirt, black Wranglers, black boots and his stetson.

Weakly she thought they would make good-looking babies. Isaiah's father wouldn't win a beauty contest between him and a rhino. But Roman? Next to him every other man looked soft. She already wanted to jump back in bed with him.

He came back with a plastic bag, opening her side and handing it to her. Her stomach turned at the sight of the purple-and-white box that held the Plan B pill.

"You alright?" he asked her quietly. She turned over the box, reading the directions.

"I'm just wondering what would have happened if I had this six years ago," she said. "I didn't even know this thing existed. But it would have been too late anyway I guess. I didn't find out I was pregnant with Isaiah until weeks after..." She trailed off, slamming a lid down on the memory.

Roman tugged a curl dangling from her pineapple. "Serena."

She looked up. He said, "I'd look after you and any child we have. I meant what I said. You'll always be protected. You're a good mother to Isaiah and I trust you'll be good to any child we make together. If anything came from what we're doing, I would take care of it. You know that, right?"

She nodded. "But what? I can hear a 'but'."

"You're young. You got ambition, plans. I can't ask you to stay up in my house barefoot and pregnant. I ain't such a selfish bastard, I hope."

"And what about your daughter? She might not want to share you."

Around his eyes went tight. "I've asked Katie to come home a dozen times. She's made her choice. I'll support her always regardless of what happens with you and me. But you don't need to worry about her."

"I wish I could tell the future," Serena said, turning the box over in her lap.

"Hell, shug, so do I." He kissed her softly, his hand going under her skirt so his thumb brushed against her aching clit. "You're so soft," he murmured.

"I'm gonna be walking into the bank with no panties on," she chided him.

"That make you wet?"

"A little."

He slid his thumb inside her, right there in the parking lot. He slowly thrust up to the knuckle until her breathing grew ragged.

"Somebody's gonna see us."

"Shhh."

"Roman? We're in *public*."

He huffed a laugh. "This dress is doing things to me." He slipped his thick finger out of her pussy.

"Yellow. I'll be damned," he murmured.

After the drug store came the DMV. Serena sat in the uncomfortable vinyl chair, wishing she had her panties back. Roman held her hand and nibbled on her fingers as he scrolled through his phone, his brow furrowed in concentration. He seemed unable to stop touching her.

"What are you doing?" she whispered, looking up from her book.

"Planning how to take care of Curley. It's got to be tonight, so after I drop you at home I'll have to head out and do this."

Oh.

"Number eight-seven-five," the speakers grated out. The official pointed at Serena.

"Knock 'em dead," said Roman. "It's the permit test, so it's basically impossible to fail," he assured her.

Shaking her head, she went up to the booth and sat down. The last time I took a test was in high school. A million years ago. She guessed every question, wondering how many traffic laws she'd seen Roman break just driving around Florin. Even Mrs. Loving seemed to play fast and loose with the rules. Serena finished up and turned in the sheet.

The official was another black woman. "Is that your man, baby?" she asked Serena.

"Yeah."

"You don't sound so sure. Can I have him?"

Serena grinned. "No, he's spoken for."

The woman looked Roman up and down, eyes twinkling. "Nevermind. I don't know if I could handle all that."

"He ain't as scary as he looks, I swear."

The woman fed the paper into a machine and waited. A green light flashed, and she chuckled. "Good job, country girl. You passed."

They stopped at a fancy breakfast place to eat, but Serena could hardly look at her delicious, maple-syrup-soaked, powdered-sugar-sprinkled French toast. She was too busy admiring her new love: her debit card. As of today, her "salary" from Roman sat in a brand new account that belonged to who? Serena Jones!

She looked up, smiling, and saw Roman smiling back. A black curl fell over his forehead and he looked sexy and adorable.

He's happy just making me happy.

"So what's it gonna be now, lil' bit?" He teased, eyeing the plastic card. "Gold watch? Pet tiger? A hundred pairs of shoes?"

"Hmm, I was thinking just a private jet."

She finished her lemonade and after an idle look around the restaurant she observed, "You know, we're the only black folks in here."

"You think they can tell?"

"For you? Probably not. White folks can never tell." She hesitated. "Roman, can I ask you something?"

"Yeah, sure."

"You got something against black people or what?"

"What? No."

When Roman lied the tips of his ears turned red. "You're lyin'. Just tell me," she urged.

"Why? So you can call me ignorant?"

"Well, I'm Black, Roman, and so is Isaiah." *And so are you, even if you won't admit it.* Roman's mother must have been a light skinned woman for Roman to pass so well. "We both might need to know if you hate our kind."

"I don't *hate* anybody. And anyway, Isaiah ain't Black," Roman said.

"What is he, then?"

"He's nothing. He's a McCall."

"Can't he be both?" she demanded.

"Let's just eat, Serena."

"I ain't scared of an opinion, Roman."

"Neither am I."

"Then just say it. Say what's on your mind. I won't judge," she prodded.

"Alright," said Roman, deciding to play ball. "Imagine all your life you only heard one perspective about a thing. Everybody just repeatin' the same lines over and over. And it went doubly hard for me because I was marked. A half-breed."

"Like Isaiah."

"So you agree he ain't Black," Roman pointed out swiftly.

Serena waved the spoon like a schoolteacher. "Isaiah's half by blood, but if other black folks accept him, then he's black. And right now I'm the only 'black folks' in his life so he's whatever I say he is."

"That's crazy."

"Well, so is you running around like you're white, Roman."

He scowled. "None of it makes sense, if you think about it," Serena continued quickly, taking some of the sharpness from her voice. "Nobody's sayin' you got to wear a sticker claiming one thing or another. We're just all living in this mess somebody else created. White folks told us we're black, and we can't go here and we can't do this. What's 'black' mean, anyway? Are we just who white folks say we are? Or something else? And what, then?" She pushed a piece of French toast around her plate. "You know, my Aunt Eulie tried to buy a house in Florin for years. She had the money, good credit and everything, but nobody wanted to sell to her. It seems like every time somebody from Black Florin tried to get ahead, someone on your side would hammer 'em down. I don't know why we can't just live together and treat each other like human beings. It's our home, too. I don't see why the McCalls should run everything." She fell silent abruptly.

"You count your Uncle Ray among those tryin' to get ahead?" Roman asked her quietly.

“No. Uncle Ray was a bastard, but most black folks aren’t mean like him just like every McCall isn’t like Curley. Most are just trying to make it and provide for their families.”

“None of them came to help you. You were up there on Pike Hill getting abused, and none of them did a damned thing for you. And you defend them?”

“I don’t blame ‘em,” said Serena frankly. “Everybody was scared to cross Bubba and his old violent drunk ass. You McCalls have a reputation on our side, if you weren’t aware. I blame *them* for not stopping their kin from abusing me. That’s who I blame. Well, except for you, I mean,” she added hastily.

Roman seemed lost in thought. She had expected him to start backing off the subject, but he actually appeared to take in her words seriously. She sensed he’d wanted to have this conversation with her for a while.

“I know White Florin ain’t full of angels,” Roman said slowly. “But it’s hard not to feel like some people are just born to lead, and others are born to serve, when everybody says it’s just and good, and it works out in your favor most of the time. I was always told Black Florin wasn’t good for nothing. And that was the polite version.”

“And you believed it?”

“Yeah. I did,” he confessed, his dark eyebrows lifting. “But I started looking into some things people were saying. All these different assumptions, stories, whatever. I even dug up some books. And I learned a lot of things. One thing being that the runoff from our fields has been pouring into Black Florin for thirty years. And let me tell you, Serena, it’s just the tip of a massive goddamned iceberg. An iceberg of shit."

"My Lord."

"I called up someone from the valley to look at it, but I fear the damage is done. Pisses me off. So that's one thing I need to fix, and soon. " He shook his head. "Yet the very suggestion of helping Black Florin has my people up in arms. They hate difference just for the sake of hating somethin'. There's no reason behind it."

"I think it's time things change," Serena said flatly.

"I agree. But it's no easy thing, changing people's ways."

Serena traced the scars on his knuckles with her fingertips. "Would your family ever accept you being with me?"

He closed his fingers around hers. "I'll make them accept it."

"What if they don't?"

"Then we'll take your private jet somewhere nice and sunny..."

She laughed, but in the back of her mind she noticed how he had avoided the question. It confirmed to Serena what she already knew: she would have to let Roman go eventually. There could be no babies, nothing but a clean and simple break. She didn't belong in his world, and she wasn't even sure she *wanted* to belong there. She had no faith his family would ever come around to seeing her as an equal. They didn't see *him* that way, and he was one of them! No, some things couldn't change in Florin, no matter how bad you wished it.

. . .

Roman's loud curse ripped Serena out of her trance. She'd been staring at the rushing scene of pine forest outside the window. She grabbed the seat for dear life as the truck braked violently, spinning out on the road.

"What is it?"

"Trouble," said Roman. He threw the Pegasus in reverse and, in a maneuver that brought them dangerously close to soaring off the mountain, turned tail.

Serena looked through the rearview mirror. And screamed. A moment later a bullet exploded the back windshield. Roman floored the gas. The Pegasus tore back down the mountain.

"Serena, the glove box," Roman said, supernaturally calm. "Open it."

She slammed the glove box and took out his gun, checking for the clip. "It's loaded."

He drives around with a loaded gun. Lord.

"I know. Hand it to me."

She did. Roman set it in his lap and whipped the wheel around, glancing quickly in the rearview. "Fucking bastards. They got my tail."

"Roman." She couldn't breathe. "What do I do?"

"You can't do nothing. Keep your head down and try not to puke."

The deafening noise rattled her to her bones. Behind them, every engine that could ride in Snatch Hill hounded them down the mountain.

Roman said, “Call my brother. Call Rebel.”

Serena scrabbled under the console and pulled out Roman’s phone. Her shaking hands could barely navigate the screen. She hit REBEL’s number and waited.

“Hello?” came a deep voice that sounded exactly like Roman.

She hit SPEAKER.

“Rebel, we have a situation,” Roman said in a very calm voice.

“What situation? We better not have a goddamned situation. I’m in Pine Crest,” Rebel replied. “Minnie’s at a doctor’s appointment. What’s going on? Sounds like Talladega over there.”

“That’s because half of Snatch Hill is trying to run me down.”

“What?”

“Curley is trying to run me off the road, brother.”

“Fuck,” Rebel replied. “Go to Larry’s.”

“Wrong side of the mountain. I was in Rowanville.”

“Cut through the foothills, then. Try Chick’s place. Doggone it, Roman, of all the fuckin times–”

“Hang up,” said Roman to Serena.

Serena ended the call. “Who else–who can we?”

"Saverin. Any of the Bailey brothers. Hurry."

They were in the foothills. Roman blew through a red light and nearly T-boned a sedan coming in the other direction. Cursing, he swerved wildly down into a shallow-sloping holler and killed the engine. The stink of rubber was terrible.

"You call them yet?" he snapped.

"Your phone is dead," said Serena hollowly.

Roman fished in the glove box for his extra battery pack. But these damn things always took a minute to boost up the charge. He watched the little green light flash in the battery pack but the phone screen remained black.

He looked down at Serena. "Hey." He put a hand on the back of her head. "It's okay. You alright?"

"Yeah. Isaiah... Roman. What if..." She could hardly say it.

He kissed her hair. "It's fine. We'll try another way. Everything will be fine, alright?"

"Can I have my panties back?"

He huffed a laugh and fished them from his pocket. "Here."

"What do we do now?" she asked as she rolled the little fabric up her legs.

Roman rubbed his jaw. "There are other routes into the mountain but it'll be slow going. If there's one ambush, there'll be more. We'll have to gamble. Choose a route Curley ain't familiar with, or won't expect me to take." Roman scowled. "If we head through the back hills, we can get to the Baileys. They'll have firepower. I reckon we're in for a hell of a day, regardless."

"Lord have mercy. What if they attack your hill?"

"That's a possibility," Roman said.

The sound of a backfiring engine in the distance made them both flinch. They pulled out of the holler, Roman tensely watching the road for any disturbance. Down the opposite direction now, circling the edge of the mountain. Long minutes passed in silence. Serena was obviously thinking about Isaiah. Roman thought about Katie. *I wish I hadn't fucked it up so bad. I'm sorry, Katie-bug.*

The sun vanished behind the mountains as they crept into the back hills. Serena eyed the gas gauge nervously. The Pegasus's mighty engine could hold a lot, and half a tank remained. But if Curley might very well chase them through the hills all night.

And we only have one gun.

Serena didn't rate her and Roman's chances right now, but all her concern went to Isaiah and Mrs. Loving. They'd left the pair safe in Roman's house. She could only hope they were safe and hidden, since she had a feeling Curley was going to cover all his bases this time.

The back hills loomed ahead. A broken, ugly scar on Florin's Western side where people wandered in and didn't wander back out. Confederate flags rose from trailers that sagged in the middle. Broken chain-link fences spilled out of the rusted hulls of cars. Everything looked smudged in gray and baked to a finish by an unforgiving sun. Only juniper trees tolerated the poisonous soil here; runoff from coal mines, now abandoned, had bled all life from the hills. Roman kept the gun in his lap, his eyes constantly moving between the channel of trailers and shambledown houses. Men raised their heads as the Pegasus roared past amid a cloud of yellow dust. Serena saw no women.

The dwellings thinned out until only a thin strip of road piled with bricks and trash remained. Roman made several right turns one after the other and steered the truck into what seemed like a ditch enveloped by the forest canopy. The truck complained up the partly washed-out road, grinding its way through aggressive branches and jutting stones. Serena bounced and jolted in the seat while Roman rode out each bump like a bull rider in the saddle.

At the edge of a wide ravine the two-track became unnavigable. They got out of the Pegasus, Roman dialing the Baileys as soon as his phone hit charge.

No signal.

"Motherfuck. We'll have to walk, Serena."

"How far are we from your hill?"

"Far. We got to reach the Bailey place first."

They hiked a mile through dense, unforgiving brush before they reached the edge of a mowed pasture. Serena winded herself trying to keep up with Roman's long strides, but worry for Isaiah gave her the strength to keep moving.

A cry from the top of the hill alerted them. Saverin Bailey trotted down the slope, a double-barrel shotgun balanced on his shoulder. "Roman, that you?" he called.

"Yeah it's me. That's Sam's older brother," he explained to Serena before turning to Saverin. She recalled that Sam was the one who had stayed back to watch their hill.

"You got an idea what the fuck is going on? I leave for one morning and Curley's got the whole mountain deadlocked," Roman said angrily.

"It ain't just Curley and the Snatch Hills," said Saverin. "He's banded with the Green Trees. They blockaded off the warehouses and they're asking for you. "

"Shit."

"I know. A buddy from the back hills hit my line about you coming," Saverin said, glancing at Serena. "I wager Curley got the memo. He's got spies out there too. He might try to come roust you out of here, so best we get inside. I called for some more men, just in case."

Roman switched into Commander mode and began firing questions at Saverin about guns and ammunition and which road led where. Serena could hardly keep up with it. *Isaiah*, she thought, with a deep hollow pain in her chest. *He's coming for Isaiah. I know it.*

And she turned out to be right. An hour later, Serena watched numbly as men trooped in and out of the house. McCall men, hardened men, some tattooed and pierced, others scarred and dusted up with yellow back hills dirt, all of them armed to the teeth. All seemed more concerned with Curley and the Green Trees bulldogging the weed fields than the fate of her child. In fact, Serena's very presence seemed to agitate them. They'd heard the rumors about Roman's new toy, the little witch who put the curse on Curley and had Roman McCall wrapped around her finger. Serena would have worried for Roman if not for the news that came shortly after they arrived at the Bailey place.

One of the Bailey men, looking through binoculars, saw cousin Eliza Jane coming up the hill waving a white rag. The Snatch Hill woman was allowed to proceed to the farmhouse. From her flushed face and annoyed expression, she'd been walking for a minute. "Where's Roman at?" she snapped.

Roman met her. She handed him a folded piece of printer paper. "I was told to give this straight to you," she grumbled. "And I'll be needing a ride back down to my job, thank you very much."

"Did Curley give this to you?"

"Yes. You better handle this shit, Roman. Sheriff Lucky's talking about bringing the state law up here."

"What's the note say?" Saverin Bailey demanded.

Roman carefully opened the folded paper. A lock of soft kinky hair tumbled to the floor.

The room swung before Serena's eyes. The next thing she knew Saverin was holding her by the elbow. At a signal from Roman, he led her out of the room and into a different, quieter one with a bed and a nightstand. With a look of brief sympathy, he set her in a chair and shut the door between her and the now-squabbling McCalls.

For a man who rarely spoke above a monotone, Roman could pitch his voice to a brassy roar that brought every man to attention. The arguing choked off and then the thunder of boots shook the floorboards under Serena's feet.

She barely heard a word or felt a thing.

A couple minutes later the door of the room opened. Roman knelt in front of her.

"Serena. It's gonna be alright."

"I want to see the note," she said.

Roman handed it to her with what they had folded up inside. No doubt the hair came from Isaiah. Just that morning she'd run her hands through his soft curls and promised to be back soon. Shaking like a leaf, she spread open the folded paper and read what it said.

Curley stated his demands plainly. He wanted either Roman McCall or Serena Jones in exchange for Isaiah. If no Serena, Isaiah would die, and the Snatch Hills would burn the warehouses full of their yearly harvest, and take control of the most profitable fields.

Roman said, "Curley's been using the train tracks to get pills from out of state. He can make the others an offer to take over the business. The Green Trees are on board, and that doesn't look good. If more take his side, Curley will run me off the mountain and there's nothing I can do. You're just a pawn in this. It's a power play he's making for control of the trade."

Just a pawn.

"None of those men out there give a damn what happens to you and Isaiah, but I do. I'm telling you I won't let Curley do shit. Alright?"

"If it's me he wants, he can have me."

"So all of Snatch Hill can rape you to death?" Roman snapped. "Nothing doing. Your ass will be right here while I handle this."

"You said you'd kill him. You were too late. Now Isaiah might be dead."

"He ain't dead. Curley won't hurt the boy." Roman stroked her thigh, trying to calm her down. "I'll own that I failed, Serena. I should have acted sooner. I should have taken his ass out last night."

You convinced him not to, said the nasty voice in her head. *You stopped him from killing Curley. It's your fault.*

"The Green Trees sided with him because I wouldn't give you up. They think we're part of some agenda from Black Florin."

"Of course," said Serena bitterly.

"I don't give a fuck. Curley gets nothing. Alright?"

She wasn't comforted. "You all let these Snatch Hills run half the mountain, not caring who they hurt. Why do you think Curley got so bold?" She wiped her forehead with the back of her hand. "I don't want to hear it. You told me your hill was safe. But nowhere is safe around you McCalls. And now my son is in danger. I was blind."

"Serena–"

"You don't know how this feels. You let your daughter run off and you didn't do nothing. I should have known better than to trust a man who wouldn't lift a finger for his own blood–"

"What the fuck are you talking about?" Roman's face tightened in rage. "While my kin are out there demanding I throw you to these wolves, see that I'm here tellin' you I love you, that I'd fight to my last breath before I let Isaiah die. Remember that Curley would be dead by now if you hadn't dragged me from that window." He looked down at her coldly. "I understand you're upset. You'll stay here where you're safe. Eliza and the women will look after you until I'm back." Then Roman left her sitting there, returning to his room full of men. Serena got up and started pacing the room, her fists opening and closing with a need to do *something*. What? She was miles away from Roman's hill, trapped in a stranger's house, with no way to contact Curley. Roman would force her to stay here while he went to "handle" the situation.

But Serena didn't trust anyone, not even Roman, to put Isaiah first. Only a mother could do that. She knew Curley would kill her son without hesitation if he didn't get what he wanted.

He wants me. He wants me to cure him.

Voices rose and fell in the other room. It would seem the McCalls didn't agree with Roman's stubborn refusal to give her up. Roman might be looking at the bigger picture, but that was Roman. He was a big-picture kind of man. To the rest of the McCalls, they saw this as just another man-woman affair got out of hand. Why shouldn't Roman give her up, if it meant Curley and the Green Trees would back down from their threat? Besides, the Snatch Hills had prior claim to Serena. It was Roman who stole her first.

Serena saw the clear path forward. She needed to save Isaiah, and needed to do so as fast as possible.

She opened the door and stepped right out into the room. His men fell silent immediately. She ignored Roman's scary look. "I volunteer to give myself up to Curley. It's me he wants. He can have me if he lets Isaiah go," she said.

"Saverin," said Roman through his teeth. "Remove her."

"Mister Bailey, think about it," Serena said quickly. "They got your brother Sam up on Roman's hill, don't they? You can deliver me and see if he's alright. I agree to give myself up to Curley if he agrees to free my son. Right? It's my *choice.*"

Saverin stopped and looked at Roman. "Now hold on," he said.

"See, Roman?" said a cousin in a loud and angry tone. "The girl don't even want to be here. She wants to go back to Curley, so let her."

Everybody looked at Roman to see how he would take this remark.

"You're right, Elian, " said Roman, narrowing his eyes. "If that's what you want, Serena, then it seems like we've solved our problem. Saddle up, boys. Let's go give Curley his show."

The crew began moving out. At the door Roman caught Serena's elbow and said in a voice laced with anger, "Let's hope you don't regret this, sweetheart."

"Don't be angry with me, Roman. You would have done the same thing."

"I won't turn you over to him."

"You might have to. So get over yourself. This is my decision." She jerked from his grip and went outside. *Deep breaths.* She'd save Isaiah, no matter what. She just hoped Roman wouldn't do anything crazy.

Before they left the Bailey place Roman took his cousin Saverin aside. Saverin said, "I don't see how we'd get to Curley without offerin' her up. Either that or we're looking at a war."

"I might have an idea."

Saverin frowned. Roman explained himself in the briefest detail, ignoring the look of horror that spread across Saverin's face the longer he talked. "Find me three honest men, and we can do it," Roman finished grimly.

"Roman. That ain't no kind of plan," laughed Saverin in disbelief.

"Ain't it? Curley's only working with the Green Trees because he has to. He knows they're just a bunch of lazy cowards. Curley's sold them a bag of goods, but at the first sign that we're threatening their own hill, Hogs and his piglets will scurry. That'll disrupt Curley-- he'll lose his temper and the whole thing will break down before we even set foot on that hill."

"Curley might hurt his hostages."

"His only leverage? I doubt that."

Saverin still looked unsure. "But ain't we the good guys? Since when do the good guys go around starting fires? Roman, it's the *harvest*. That's all our dope for the year."

"We can't grow bud forever, Sav." Though they were pressed for time, Roman shared what he'd learned investigating the water situation in Black Florin. "The earth near Green Tree Hill is bad. All the Snatch Hill meth shit, maybe, but there's other things that come blowing in there from the back hills. We need to clear new fields or take the business in some other direction. Or we'll have nothing when the real trouble comes."

"All that work we did in the harvest. All for nothing."

"If Curley wins today, is that a future you want to live in? This is a necessary sacrifice."

Saverin nodded slowly. "How will this go down, then?" He murmured, glancing around to make sure the others didn't overhear them. "You want me to head over there now?"

"As soon as you can. Make sure you ain't seen–and pick your men wisely."

"I got cousins on Snatch Hill that ain't too pleased with Curley's little dictatorship. But they'd want compensation." He glanced at Roman.

"I'll compensate. Just get it done."

They clasped hands. Saverin hesitated before adding, "I'm counting on you to help Sam. He's a big boy, and I know he can handle himself, but you know... He's my baby brother."

"I'll get him back safe," Roman promised. "You have my word."

CHAPTER 13
THE KING IN HIS CASTLE

Curley couldn't wait to get his hands on that little bitch. Oh, he just couldn't wait. He put his feet up on Roman McCall's desk and opened drawers until he found the special whiskey the big uppity bastard liked to savor for himself. Pouring himself a generous glass, he swilled the amber liquid around before he took himself a nice deep drink.

"Fuckin right," he cursed appreciatively, refilling the glass as soon as he drained it. At least the halfbreed had taste. He recognized the flavor as one of Uncle Jodie's specialties. Fuck Uncle Jodie. Bastard. The old man ran a still in the back hills and made the best whiskey for miles. A long time since Curley had had a taste of Uncle Jodie's brew. That was because Jodie refused point blank to sell to any Snatch Hills, on account of Bubba dishonoring one of his daughters some years back. As if the slut hadn't asked for it.

"You ever miss him, Jessomy?" Curley asked his younger brother, rifling through another drawer in the desk.

"Miss who?" said Jessomy stupidly.

"Bubba. Our dear old big brother. You ever miss him?"

"No," said Jessomy. "No, I can't say I do, Curley."

"You was always plotting on Serena," Curley sneered. "That's why. You couldn't wait 'till Bubba was toes-up so you could have a turn under her dress."

"Good thing I didn't," said Jessomy boldly. "Because she turned your dick limp as a newt."

Curley casually pointed his revolver at his brother. "Watch your mouth, Jesso-boy," Curley said. "I've a mind to paint them walls with your guts like I did that Bailey son of a bitch." He laughed as Jessomy went green. Though it turned his own stomach some, thinking about how Sam Bailey collapsed when the bullet ripped through his jawbone. Fell like a box of eggs, whimpering like a baby the whole time. Well, good riddance. Sam had always been a self-important jackass, one of Roman's stooges, a rat and a snitch. Just like all the Baileys. Uppity. If there was one thing Curley McCall hated, it was them who took notions of greatness with nothing to back it up.

"Quit pointing that gun at me," Jessomy complained.

"Snatch Hill ain't nothing to be fucked with," Curley said, to nobody in particular. "I'm the ruler of these hills, boy." He lowered the revolver to root through a different drawer in Roman's desk, discovering a second prize: a box of cubans. Curley slit the seal on the box with his switchblade and dug out the fattest one. He packed the end in with his thumb. "Light me," he ordered his brother.

Jessomy held out the lighter.

"Don't worry, Jesso. I got plans for us. Big plans."

"I'd like to see Roman McCall pushing daisies before I hear talk of plans."

"Chicken shit," Curley accused. Though Jessomy was right. As soon as he had Serena in hand, Curley planned to dispose of Roman McCall quickly.

"I'm feeling pretty damned good right now, Jessomy. We're going to be runnin' pills and dope through every fuckin' hill far as the eye can see," Curley said, warmed by the idea of Roman dying. "We'll get ourselves a tidy operation. And those boys down the mountain will see what's good. They're just waiting for us to tie this hog, and then we'll be right as rabbits. I got it all figured out. Leave it to big brother."

"You don't need Serena for all of that," Jessomy sulked. "I reckon your dream was lyin'. You don't need to fuck her to make it stand straight."

"Not that bullshit again," Curley snapped. Jessomy's annoying attachment to the girl drove him crazy. "I'm gonna tear up that little cunt 'till she can't walk straight. Then you can have her. Whatever's left of her, anyway." Curley fingered the cross around his neck, nervous and excited. Some might call him superstitious, but he always followed messages from dreams. They gave him visions, same as the men from the Bible. A dream told him he needed to fuck Serena to make his dick work. And a dream was to thank for this latest scheme — a stroke of genius, playing Roman against that little bitch. Two birds, one stone.

But how can you fuck her if it ain't rising in the first place? Every smart-ass wanted to know that. Well, Curley chalked up his last failed attempts to bed Serena as a matter of ill-timed interruptions. He wouldn't make that mistake again. No; he'd get inside the girl even if it took all night.

Bubba kept the girl as his personal slave for nearly a year. Waiting on him hand and foot. Warming his bed. She was pretty and soft, always running and hiding, which attracted Curley, who was used to more whorish types. Curley begged his brother for a go at Serena, but Bubba was just a territorial bastard. Been like that since they were boys. Curley was right sick of his greedy ass. So one night he slipped a little something in Bubba's stout, then dragged the girl in the back room and did the deed.

Not worth it, in hindsight. Bubba whooped his ass, and the girl turned out to be a miserable lay. She cried and fought the whole time, and then she laid that fucking hex on him. Overnight Curley went from a swaggering stallion to a limp-dick laughingstock. It was all Serena's fault, and Bubba's too, for not softening the girl up to Curley.

Anyway, Curley would soon get his dues. He puffed on the cigar. The smoke made his excited blood run hot. He could feel his hands around Serena's throat already. He could feel her squeezing him as he forced himself inside her. He'd leave her dead and bleeding. Jessomy could have her, then. Better hurry and get a fuck on her before she got stiff.

Curley sized up his little brother with a familiar dislike. Bug-eyed little pissant. Jesso went running his mouth to Roman about Serena and started all this trouble in the first place; the little fucker was lucky Curley had such a forgiving nature. But it worked out, didn't it? Jesso's betrayal gave

Roman McCall the shovel to dig his own grave. People thought he'd lost his mind. To think the halfbreed would get so attached to Serena he'd let the clan fall just to have her? That was almost funny.

In the end, Roman's obsession with the girl did Curley's work for him. The Green Trees had an almost supernatural terror of black folks. Family legend told the Green Tree patriarch, in slavery times, had lynched all five sons of a local negro family. In revenge their grandmother, a supposed witch, cursed the whole Green Tree bloodline. The details differed depending on who was telling that particular story.

Curley thought it was a load of shit, personally, but generations later the Green Trees were jumpy about anything to do with witches, negroes, and curses. Roman's involvement with a girl who could cast hexes on virile men just wound them up. It took nothing for Curley to convince the fools they could arrange a little coup d'état. With Roman dead, the Green Trees could have complete control of the drug trade off their hill. They could even partner with the Snatch Hills, their neighbors. Less darkies, more money. Simple as that. Of course Curley had no intention of working with the idiotic Green Trees. But without Roman's force behind them, those fat asses would be sitting ducks. Once they helped him get rid of Roman, Curley would set about removing every Green Tree from his side of the mountain. Divide and conquer.

Curley blew smoke rings at the rafters and smiled. He felt like a king already. He was barely a day away from running the whole mountain root to tip. All thanks to Jessomy's big mouth. Jessomy, like many dunces, had a knack for stumbling his way into fortune. Curley figured he might just keep the little idiot around for a while after all.

Suddenly the study doors slammed open. Jessomy gave a stupid yelp of surprise that made Curley immediately reconsider shooting him, but Hogs Green Tree's racket captured his attention.

"Curley, they torched us!" bawled Hogs. "The whole mountain's up in flames!" No sooner did he make this outburst than his nephew Gump pushed past him. "Roman McCall's coming," Gump huffed. "He's got the Baileys and the Steeles as backup."

"Fuck Roman!" Hogs shouted. "We got a fuckin' inferno on our hands!"

"What are you apes yellin' about?" Curley felt jittery from the cigar and in no mood for Green Tree bullshit. "Ain't you supposed to be watching my prisoners?"

"Look, you little weasel," Hogs growled, leaning over the desk and stabbing a thick finger at the window. "See that?"

Curley rocked back in the chair and opened the blinds. Dumb fuckin' Green Trees... He blinked. The chair slammed back to the floor. "What the fuck?" he yelped.

"I told you," said Hogs furiously. "Now what the hell is goin' on?"

Curley's cellphone rang. He pounced on it, dropping the lit cigar in his haste. It began spewing embers all over the carpet; he kicked it aside.

"Johnce?"

"Curley!" His cousin Johnce's howl shot through the speakers. "Curley, the fuckin' lab–it blew up–" coughing swallowed his next words.

Four men stared out the window of Roman's study in growing horror. Plumes of smoke rose from the direction of Snatch Hill and its Green Tree neighbors. Curley stumbled to his feet and pushed past Jessomy, who was gaping like a landed trout.

Curley barked into the phone, "What the fuck do you mean it blew up, Johnce?"

"The whole thing just exploded. I don't know! Can't see... Can't breathe..."

"Nevermind it!" Curley said abruptly. "Get as much out of there as you can, Johnce. That cargo ain't my shit to lose. You hear me? You let those crates go up, it's your ass!"

"But Curley," Johnce choked. "Curley, the whole thing's afire. There ain't no savin' nothing."

"Anybody inside?" Curley stalked down the hall, his boot heels thundering on the hardwood. Somebody had to be responsible. Somebody was going to pay.

"M-my brother," Johnce wailed. "Oh God. He's still in there–"

"I don't give a fuck about your brother. Get my damned stash out! These Rowanville fucks will fry us all if you don't save it!" Curley screamed. He hung up and raked a hand through his hair.

Too convenient. Too fuckin' convenient.

"I'll go rally the men," Gump said grimly to his brother. Hogs nodded. "You do that. Make it snappy."

"This is Roman's doing," Curley heaved, storming towards the bedroom where Serena's brat and the nanny were imprisoned. "I'll gut that fucking halfbreed!"

"Roman's doing?" bellowed Hogs, grabbing Curley's shoulder with a meaty paw. "But this ain't the first time one of your little crack houses got lit up next to my hill, is it? I'm liable to think it's regular Snatch Hill negligence we have here." The older man shook his phone in Curley's face. "The fire's spreading to my fields! I can't be up here playin' cowboys and indians with you boys. We're leaving."

Curley sneered. "What a surprise. A Green Tree turning tail. Damned cowards, the pack of ye. Don't you see? Roman did this to distract us."

"Then I'll kill Roman McCall some other time, when my hill ain't fixin' to go up in smoke," Hogs said. "And I dare you to call me yellow again, you putrid little jackal. You Snatch Hills got more rot than week-old catfish."

Green Tree and Snatch Hill men bristled at once.

Curley said, "Pardon?"

"You heard me, boy. Unless your ears need cleanin'? I'd be happy to oblige."

"Only thing needing cleanin' is that tub of grease under your ribs," Curley sneered. "When was the last time you swept under that thing?"

"Mind your tongue, boy. I was crackin' the marrow out of uppity little boys before you was shitting green," Hogs growled.

"Tough talk's all you're good for, you fat sack of shit," Curley said, his temper rising. "Lord, I never could stand a Green Tree. And ain't you just the loudest, dumbest bastard that ever dragged his knuckles off that fuckin' hill, *Hogs*."

"I hope Roman sticks you like a worm, Curley McCall. You and your poisonous kin."

Curley drew his revolver. "Go on and get, then. Yellow-belly!"

The atmosphere in the hall became lethal. "Point a gun at me, will ye?" Hogs roared, brandishing his own pistol. "I knew we was wrong to trust your schemin' hide. Wouldn't surprise me if you lit them fires yourself to force us to sell your little pills. Never trust a Snatch Hill!"

"One Snatch Hill is worth ten of your'n," called a man from Curley's side. "Fuckin' Green Trees! Bunch of lard-assed, buck-toothed–"

"Sister fuckers," Curley finished.

"Limp dick," said Hogs brutally.

The house erupted.

Roman, arriving on his hill, confronted a scene of utter chaos. Smoke poured from the windows of his study, flames reaching through the shattered glass to thirstily taste the air. Just feet away from Sam Bailey's lifeless corpse, Snatch Hills and Green Trees brawled openly in the front yard, with Curley McCall nowhere to be seen.

Serena scrabbled at her seatbelt.

“What the hell are you doing?”

“I’m going in there,” she said.

“The hell you are!” He stretched across the console and hauled her back into the seat before a hail of gunfire turned up the dirt in front of them. An automatic. Fucking Christ. A gun like that would turn Serena to pink mist before his eyes.

“Get down, Serena, damn it!” He hauled the Winchester from the backseat. “Don’t fucking move from this car.”

“Isaiah’s in there, Roman!”

“I know,” he said. “If we just–”

She jumped out of the truck and took off in a sprint towards the house.

“Fuck! Damn it– SERENA!” A blur of seconds, panic, and he landed practically on top of her. They tumbled to the ground.

Bullets raged above their heads. She cried out in pain. Roman rolled off her but still covered her body with a protective arm. “Ouch,” she sobbed.

The shooter was pausing to reload. “You hurt? Nevermind —GO! GO!”

She scrambled up without wasting a second to reply, and charged towards the house. He chased after her and hauled her into the shelter of the garage awning. Ten seconds to catch their breath. Bailey men poured from the trees, but the bastard shooting from above drove them back. Roman's heart pounded like a steel-driver's hammer. He and Serena were lucky to be alive.

They rounded the house and stopped again, for now out of sight from the automatic. Roman loaded his borrowed Winchester as fast as his shaking hands allowed. "You damned stubborn– what the fuck were you thinking?" he roared at her, apoplectic. "You could have died!"

Serena clutched her left arm. Sweat poured down her face. "Isaiah's in there. Roman, I have to get inside."

"You won't be good to him if that shooter turns you into swiss cheese. Fuck." He glanced up towards the plume of smoke coming from his home. Not good. "They could be keeping him in the guest house," he muttered, reasoning out loud.

"No," said Serena, "If your house is burning, and he's inside, we'd be wasting time checking the guest house first. I have to go in."

Her voice sounded strained. Roman glanced at her arm. Also not good. He remembered hearing a cracking sound as he landed on top of her. *Fuck.*

He faced the burning house and the ugly choice before him. Running into burning buildings was nearly always a fatal mistake, but he couldn't let Isaiah die.

I couldn't keep my promise to Saverin. I'll keep it to her.

He touched Serena's hand. "Get one of the Baileys' attention, but keep out of sight."

Her eyes widened as she realized what he intended. "Hell no. I'm coming in with you!" she cried.

"Your arm's broken. You go in there, you die."

"How will you get out?"

"I just will. Get somewhere safe and don't leave it. Alright? You hear me?"

"Y-yes," she said. "But—"

He turned away from her and drove in one of the lower windows with the rifle butt. Thin trails of smoke reached out of the house like tiny hands, dragging him inexorably towards the heart of the inferno. Serena grabbed his shirt with her good hand. "Roman... Thank you. Be careful." She fought back tears. "I'm sorry for what I said. Earlier."

"It'll be fine, darlin'." He tried at the last minute to find the words. "You're the best thing that ever happened to me," he managed. *And I love you.*

She kissed him quickly, clumsily, and then he was gone.

Serena backed up from the house, watching her man vanish through the window. A numb ache threaded up her left arm, but she would worry about that later. She felt like screaming and crying and pulling her hair out. How could a day unravel so fast?

What if Roman couldn't find Isaiah?

She backed up from the house and searched the windows for any sign of Mrs. Loving or her son. Her ears strained for a sound, a scream. I'm Isaiah's mother. I should know where he is. I should feel it, shouldn't I?

The horrible instinct grew. What if Isaiah wasn't in the house at all? Roman would die. Choking on smoke, or burning to death.

Her eyes fell on the gardener's shed behind the house. *A ladder*! Perfect. She knew how Roman would get out. She just had to—

"Serena."

She screamed and spun, nearly colliding into Jessomy McCall. It was like he'd appeared out of the smoke itself.

She scrambled back, putting distance between herself and this new threat. Jessomy had put on weight since she saw him last. His shirt and jeans were smudged in soot. Sweat plastered his hair to his broad forehead in lank strings. His giddy expression chilled her. "I can't believe it," he said. "It's you. You're safe."

Had he seen Roman go into the house? What did he want? He has a gun. Jessomy grabbed her shoulder, the gleeful look fading to one of concern as she cried out in pain. "Are you alright, Sarie? You're hurt. Did he hurt you?"

She stepped sideways, her heart pounding. "Don't touch me, Jessomy."

"Don't be that way, honey. I came to rescue you." Jessomy's close-set eyes watered. He licked his lips. "And I saved your boy, too."

"What?"

"Isaiah. He's back there." Jessomy jerked his head towards the woods. "I got him out while Curley was hollerin' at the Green Trees. Took him out. He's safe."

"You're lying. Isaiah's in that house! Roman went to look for him. Why are you lyin' to me?"

"I ain't lying, Sarie. I never lied to you."

"You let Curley rape me. You watched!" She screamed. "I know you did. I saw you, lookin' through a crack in the door. Sick bastard. You told me you'd protect me, and that was all lies!"

"But I'm here now," Jessomy whined. "And I saved your boy. Don't you want to see him? Come with me and we'll go get him. We'll be together."

She didn't believe him for a second. "Who's up there shooting that gun?" Serena demanded.

"Curley," Jessomy replied. "He got hold of one of Roman's guns. Green Trees chased 'im into the attic, and I got away. But you're safe. That's all I care about. My sweetheart..."

"Where's Mrs. Loving?" Serena pressed. Her eyes darted to the windows, searching for a sign of Roman. Nothing, except the smoke was getting thicker. Had Roman risked himself for nothing? The ache in her arm became a grinding agony.

"I had to leave the woman," said Jessomy. "I only got your boy out. He's just this way, Sarie. Come on. Let me tend to your arm. Get away from here."

A noise like a falling tree came from inside the house. She dry-heaved. Roman, Isaiah, Mrs. Loving... Oh Lord, am I going to lose everybody? All I can do is stand here while they burn.

"Isaiah is waiting," said Jessomy, grabbing her injured arm. His voice hardened. "Time to go."

"Ma! Ma!"

Serena's head jerked up. The blood ran backwards in her veins.

"Baby!" she screamed, forgetting Jessomy, forgetting Roman, forgetting every single piece of danger around her. She jerked out of the man's grasp and bolted towards her son. Isaiah leaned out of Roman's bedroom window, his small arms waving desperately to get her attention.

"Isie, get back inside! Don't fall!"

Her baby ducked back through the window. Her brain ran probabilities. *Roman's room has the thickest door in the house. It will protect him. I just have to get to him before the roof falls in. Oh God. How can I get him down from there?* "Isie! Isaiah! I'm coming!"

Jessomy hauled her back by the hair and slammed his gun into her temples. "No," he snarled. "No. No, Serena. Leave him. It can be just us." He pawed at her breasts, ignoring her cry of pain as he crushed her injured arm. "Just you and me. I waited so long for you. I waited to make you mine. Roman was supposed to save you for me. You're mine...Please..."

Serena bucked like a wild mare, rolling and stumbling through the grass to dislodge him. But the man just kept coming, dragging her back from the window, away from her son.

She barely knew what she screamed, or if any of her desperate punches met their target. She fought Jessomy harder than she'd ever fought anyone. She fought him with all her strength until by some miracle she broke his hold. She spun around and kicked him hard where it would hurt the most, putting everything she had into the blow.

He went down. Serena didn't hesitate; there was not one shred of pity left in her. She slammed a heel into Jessomy's free hand until she felt the bones of his fingers actually separate. She snatched his gun from where it lay in the grass and hurried towards the other side of the house. Cradling her throbbing arm while trying to balance the heavy weapon was nearly impossible. *Ignore the pain. Get to Isaiah.*

The ladder was behind the gardener's shed about a dozen yards from the guest house. But she couldn't tote the thirty-pound ladder and haul Jessomy's gun at the same time. With no waistband in her dress to hold the weapon, and only one working hand...

Can't let Jessomy have it. She tossed the weapon onto the guest house roof. Next she retrieved the ladder. Her crippled arm made her slow and clumsy, but she had to act before Jessomy got his crazy ass up and made more trouble.

One-armed she hauled the ladder against the lower part of the guest house roof and scrambled up to the sloped platform. The entirety of Roman's hill swooped before her in a dizzying rush. Bailey men poured onto the lawn, yelling and taking shots at the Snatch Hills fleeing into the trees. The blue-and-red lights of lawmen flashed in the near distance. Don't think. Don't think. Serena planted her feet on the slanted shingles and tugged at the ladder one-handed. Now both her shoulders felt like someone was popping them out of their sockets. Sweat poured down her face, stinging her eyes. *This ain't nothing. This is temporary. Don't think. Don't think. Don't fall.* She let herself scream through the pain as she dragged the ladder up beside her. She sat down hard to stop herself overbalancing.

No time to breathe. She quickly kicked off the sandals. One thing at a time. She needed to remain calm. Panic would ruin everything. She imagined taking Isaiah to the beach. Isaiah sitting on Roman's shoulders. Isaiah laughing under a Christmas tree. Isaiah depended on her now, and she wouldn't let him down ever again.

Controlling her fear with slow, deep breaths, she slammed the ladder into the narrow space between the guest house roof and Roman's balcony. Would it hold?

It would. One foot, then the other, a small jump up every rung. The ruined yellow dress fluttered around her thighs. With both arms, the whole thing might have taken less than a minute. *Don't think. Just move.*

Maneuvering over the top of the ladder to clear the balcony railing was the hardest, and she nearly lost her balance and went over the edge. She caught herself just in time, dragging her body weight over the side. Don't think. Just as the ladder began to slip sideways she caught it, like a one-armed machine, and pulled the heavy thing onto the balcony. The bones in her body were grinding together. She'd never felt so much pain in her life.

She turned to the French doors. No lights inside.

"Isaiah!" she cried, throwing herself at the glass. "Isaiah, can you hear me?"

. . .

Roman plunged through the darkness of the house, keeping his back to the wall and hunching low where the air was cleaner. House fires could burn slow or consume a place in seconds; either way, a man couldn't survive long on lungfuls of smoke. Every second was a struggle not to rush out the door and inhale the sweet fresh air; his human instinct rebelled against every step, but he'd often plunged into dangerous situations just like this, learning to master the fearful, cringing animal in every human with the cold logic of a predator.

The floor above him creaked ominously. *Somebody upstairs. Attic. Curley.*

Katie's know-it-all little voice spoke in his head. *Most people in house fires die of asphyxiation before they burn to death.* Thanks, Katie.

He climbed the short flight of stairs to the bedrooms and looked down the long hallway towards the source of the blaze. It would take time before the fire reached this end of the hall... but how long? Seconds? Minutes? He could only hope Isaiah was somewhere in the bedrooms. Otherwise the boy was likely dead. Between Roman and the heart of the fire slumped the bodies of his fallen kinsmen. Green Trees and Snatch Hills. He wouldn't be adding to the corpses in this burning tomb.

I promised her.

He checked the living room, the kitchen, every cupboard and closet. Calling for Isaiah would waste precious air, and already he felt his lungs heaving for a break. The bedrooms, then. He doubled back. A crash came from his study, turning his guts to ice water. Flames glowed around the open door like the gate to hell itself, and then he saw the strangest thing that stopped him dead in his tracks.

A carpenter bee.

It's a hallucination. Oxygen deprivation.

The little creature came twirling through the tendrils of smoke like a stray piece of ash and landed on the barrel of his Winchester. Roman blinked. "Isaiah?" he called, his voice rough and inaudible among the screaming timbers of the house. Black smoke billowed into the hall. It would be death to inhale. He watched the flames lick up the edge of a fallen man's shirt.

Roman.

Yes, Ma?

Roman, he's here. Time to leave.

I'll stay. I want to stay with you.

Go. Run. Hurry.

Ma, fight him. Please...

I can't, baby.

He checked Katie's room first, which brought him closer to the flames.

Death ain't forever, Roman. You go everywhere. You see everything. You can live in an empty bottle, or a tiny little seashell. You can fly. Imagine that, baby. Flyin' right out of this place... Going anywhere we want.

The bee buzzed angrily in the hall. Katie's room was empty. His heart broke to see everything exactly where he'd left it, which was exactly where his daughter had left it the night she ran away. He hadn't moved anything just in case she came back. *Delusional.*

On to the master bedroom. The door was cool under his palm–a good sign. He pushed at the shattered lock with the Winchester. Roman always locked his room before he left it, and that meant somebody had torn at the lock to get inside. It stood to reason they'd stashed Isaiah in there, too. He hoped he hadn't wasted too much time, but if Isaiah was in there, then he'd escape most of the smoke.

"Isaiah?" he coughed, putting his shoulder to the door.

The heavy wood panel didn't budge.

Fuck.

Someone must have piled furniture in front of it. Roman heaved at it, pushed and slammed his broad back against it. Nothing.

He almost wanted to laugh. But of course, he could barely breathe. His head hurt. He planted his feet into the floor and pushed. He pushed until his heart felt like it would burst. It was like trying to budge the mountain itself. Panting hard, Roman leaned back against the oak panel he'd carved with his own two hands. Tears stung his eyes. From the smoke. The carpenter bee landed near his head. Roman stared into its shining compound eye. *Is this it, then, my friend? Am I done?*

He threw himself against the door again.

Nothing.

Shit. Roman started to laugh. It wasn't funny, but it was.

Hearing things. Movement and crashing. "Roman?" someone called from far away. Hearing things. Hearing... He coughed and coughed into his sleeve. *Serena. I wanted to marry you... I'm sorry I was such a bastard.*

And suddenly the door swung backward, and he nearly toppled into the room.

"Roman!" Serena screamed.

He blinked up at her like a vision of an angel, but she was real. No dream. No hallucination. His woman, his life, his everything. He shoved his way in, coughing and inhaling clean air.

"Roman, I found Isaiah," she cried.

"Where..." He caught a handful of her dress and tugged her towards him.

"He's on the balcony. Oh my God... I thought you were dead. You're alive!"

"There was something... against the door."

"Mrs. Loving barred it. They tied her and Isaiah up. She got free and blocked off the room."

"Then where is she?"

Serena swallowed hard. "Over there."

Roman crossed the far side of the bed nearest to the doors and saw Mrs. Loving.

"What happened?" He asked hoarsely.

"A stroke, I think."

“My God. She didn’t deserve that.” He stared down at the poor woman, the nearest thing he’d had to a mother since his actual mother, and felt just numb. “I can’t leave her here.”

“Can you lift her?” Serena said doubtfully.

Roman hauled the old woman over his shoulders in an undignified heap and staggered out to the balcony. The fresh air and sunshine were a relief. But even after he gently placed Mrs. Loving down and crossed her arms over her breast, the weight of her never left his shoulders.

He looked up and saw Isaiah staring at him.

The boy who had cried over rabbits was gone. Isaiah looked down at Mrs. Loving and brushed away a tear from his small cheek. Roman put a hand on the boy’s head and drew Isaiah against his hip.

“It’ll be alright, son,” he murmured. “It’ll be fine.”

The bee looped off into the forest, unnoticed by anyone.

CHAPTER 14
JUST FINE

A week later, Roman McCall strode through the burned-out ruin of two hills, his face turned towards a relentless late-summer sun. Wind pushed around the smell of charred marijuana and a distinct chemical odor. The fire had not discriminated. Fields, warehouses, and even a trailer park went up in the raging inferno caused by Roman's sabotage of the Green Tree warehouses and the accidental, unrelated explosion from Curley's meth lab. The two fires, instead of banking each other, combined in strength and spread. For six hours flames torched acres of the hills and choked half the mountain on a cloud of noxious smoke. By the time state reinforcements arrived only a trail of devastation remained.

Roman's gambit had come at a steep price. The most obvious crunched beneath his feet, a year's hard work reduced to ash and smoking stumps. The human cost now huddled in the Florin Hotel, their extended visit paid for by Roman until he could find another park to house them. And his cousin Saverin now lay like a pincushion in the

Rowanville Intensive Care Unit, pumped to the gills with morphine while doctors figured out how much of his face and upper body remained from the burns.

A sharp whistle alerted the party of six as they crossed the burned-out field. They all turned as one. A stranger came up from the bluffs and headed straight towards the group.

The slower-brained put their hands near to their belts, but Roman noticed immediately the man was not from Florin, and from the way he walked and dressed, also not of their sort.

"Afternoon, gentlemen," the stranger said, flashing a white smile that didn't move any other part of his face. “Now, which one of you would be Roman McCall?"

A Suit.

"Who's asking?" grunted Roman.

“James Strangeway, Drug Enforcement.”

Roman put out a hand and the man grasped it. Calluses under the last four fingers from lifting weights, not a hammer or a plow. Roman was reminded of his brother Ross.

The man raised dark sunglasses to reveal eyes the color of dirty ice. "A pleasure to meet you, Mister McCall. Mind if we have a word?"

"Let's have it, then."

"A word alone," the agent clarified.

The rest of the group stepped aside. Strangeway didn't talk for nearly two minutes. Roman chewed his piece of hay and waited.

"I think you know why we're up here, McCall."

"Big fire," Roman observed stolidly.

"I know you'll just play dumb country boy right now. That's fine. You're a busy man, so I'll make this brief as possible."

"I appreciate that."

"You're on notice. There will be an investigation into what happened here. My professional advice would be to give nothing less than your complete cooperation."

“Of course,” said Roman, eyeing the man sidelong. *My ass.*

“We'll be in touch,” the agent smiled. “Let's hope things stay nice and quiet on this mountain for a while, eh McCall?”

“Yes, let's hope.”

They walked back to the group in thoughtful silence.

“Tip your hats to the government fella, boys,” Roman said to his cousins as Strangeway turned to leave. “We'll be seeing a lot of him from now on. Best you memorize his face so you can greet him properly in the future.”

The Agent smiled coldly at Roman before turning back up the bluff.

. . .

Serena picked up one of the cushions from the bed with her good arm and lobbed it at Roman. Though he looked fast asleep, he caught the pillow mid-air and tossed it back at her. Ha! She knew it.

She glanced down at Isaiah laying fast asleep between them before she swung her legs off the edge of the bed and quietly walked towards the door. Isaiah stirred when the old floorboards creaked but didn't rise. She left the door open for Roman as he followed her out into the cool late-summer night.

Serena liked this place. It was quiet, just a small cabin off Meadow Lake meant as a hunter's retreat. Roman said the McCalls rented it out during deer season. There seemed to be no end to the properties Roman had stashed all over the place, but she wasn't complaining. This hideout kept her safe from vengeance-seeking Snatch Hills and all the bad gossip swirling around Florin about her involvement with the McCall clan's budding turf war. It was lonely and isolated, but that was the point.

She leaned over the balcony and watched the full moon floating to the surface of the indigo lake. A chorus of crickets filled the night with music. Lightning bugs danced on the shoreline. Animals were so free; humans were the real fools who made up all these rules about who you could or couldn't love.

Roman wrapped his arms around her from behind. "Hi, angel."

"If neither of us can sleep, I figure we can take some of this nice air."

"Damn sure better than the air up in town. Whole place smells like a campfire made out of crack pipes." His chest rumbled as he spoke. "How's your arm?"

"It's alright." A hairline fracture and a sprained wrist were her only physical scars from the day of the fires. She counted herself lucky. Saverin McCall, carrying out Roman's orders, had been trapped by the spreading flames and barely escaped with his life. His face and upper body were so badly burned he was still in ICU. No one told yet him that his brother Sam was dead.

No wonder Roman wasn't sleeping. Guilt plagued him over the Bailey brothers and the trailer park that burned up, though thankfully all the people from there, unlike Sam Bailey, made it out in time. Roman had a long road ahead to put back together a mountain even more broken than before.

For the past week he'd spent his nights with Serena and his days moving supplies to families, talking to media, taking stock of the damages and making promises backed by cash or a handshake.

Somehow he found the time to get her own affairs in order, too. One day Roman turned up unexpectedly with a deed of sale for the property on Pike Hill. Isaiah now stood to inherit some money which Roman had taken pains to set up in a trust.

The hit to his finances from the fires made him uneasy about her and Isaiah's future. She was touched that he would still think about protecting her while so many other things occupied his attention, but of course that was just Roman.

What could she do to comfort him? *Nothing,* he said. *Nothing, baby girl, I'm fine.* He would never complain or make her feel bad for what had happened. Even though, Serena knew, it was because of her that he'd ended up in this position.

"I'm sending you and Isaiah away. Somewhere in the valley," he said.

"Nowhere is safer to me than by your side," she replied softly.

"It's gonna be a mess on that mountain, Serena. There's more bad blood now than when we started, and you can't get in the middle of it. Somebody could try again to take you or Isaiah to get to me. Or they'd just cut your throats. I'd need to have you watched all the time. You'd be a prisoner all over again. You don't want that." He took her hand. "Think about Isaiah."

Ever since the fires, Isaiah had bouts of nightmares just like on Pike Hill. He missed Mrs. Loving. He drew pictures of angels and talked about her constantly. *Is Mrs. Loving in heaven? Will she turn into a ghost and visit us?* Serena barely knew what to say; it took everything in her not to cry when Isaiah asked these questions.

Roman was right. Isaiah needed a fresh start somewhere stable, with children his own age. Structure and routine would help him get past the loss of his friend. So Roman argued, anyway, and Serena could not deny it. They had to leave Florin.

I can't have them both. I put Isaiah first, always.

"So what will you do, Roman?"

"I'll never stop fighting for us. I'll work hard and get it right."

"So will I."

He drew her down into one of the balcony chairs that dipped just out of sight of the bed. *Make it fast.* But she didn't want it to be fast.

She straddled him, and they embraced there for a long time just enjoying the feeling of being close. Her arm throbbed in the cast but he was careful to arrange her in a way that wouldn't disturb it. For such a big man, Roman could be so gentle.

He put kisses on her neck and rolled the nightie up over her sex. Serena sighed and raised her leg, straddling his waist. He got himself free and slid his cock inside her.

"Take it slow. Take what you need, angel."

She rolled her hips, massaging him with her soft wet insides and loosening herself up until she could sink down all the way, fitting his whole length inside her. It always hurt when she did that but in a couple strokes she found her way to an intense orgasm made sweeter from the pain. She felt full of Roman, and as he pumped against the creamy barrier of her womb she wanted to just beg him to break her. When he came, he spilled all over her stomach and thighs. He cried out and held her close. Her fingers slid in his semen as she tried to grip his wrists, spreading it where he clamped down on her flesh. She wanted to be stained by him. She would never want another man but Roman.

CHAPTER 15
EPILOGUE

THREE MONTHS LATER

"He's here!" Isaiah screamed from the window. "He's outside!"

"Who?" Serena said innocently. "Who's outside?"

"ROMAN!" Isaiah shouted.

"Roman? Isaiah, I don't know anybody named Roman."

"Ma!" Isaiah cackled. "Ma, it's *Roman- Roman.*"

"Oh, him? I never want to see that trifling man again! I should tell him to leave, right?"

"No!" Isaiah screamed, and shot out the door before his mother could stop him, laughing like a maniac.

He bowled right into Roman, who lifted the boy up and swung him around until Isaiah was breathless with glee. This way he could kiss Serena before Isaiah broke in with a million and one questions, as he always did.

Serena said shyly, tasting toothpaste on his lips, "Hi, big man."

"Hi." Roman smiled at her. She went on tiptoe for another kiss, her heart beating nervously. "You want to come inside?"

"Yeah, but we can't stay long or the fish will leave, right Isaiah? Go get your gear, son." As Isaiah sped back inside, Roman cast an assessing eye over the boy's skinny frame. "He's shot up about six inches since I saw him last," he observed.

"I know- thank God. I was afraid Pike Hill had stunted him."

"Seems like his Mama's growing in the opposite direction," Roman said, patting her ass.

"I put on a little weight, but it's nothing."

"You look beautiful," Roman said, his hand settling on her butt. "You gonna give me some of that later, right?"

"If you're very nice," she whispered. *Tell him. Tell him now.*

He squeezed her. "How nice?"

"I'm ready!" Isaiah cried, emerging from the bedroom with his tackle box and pole. A hunter's cap slipped over his eyes. It amused Serena that Isaiah, defender of small and fluffy rabbits, took to fishing like oil to cotton. "Fish aren't cute" was his reasoning. Roman took him out to one of the reservoirs near Rowanville, and they spent all day there while Serena studied.

During those times Serena missed Mrs. Loving the most. Knowing how hard the old woman had prayed for her success made her even more dedicated to pass her exams and get her education. No matter how long it took, Serena would grind it out. It was hard to find the time between waitressing and caring for Isaiah, so the days when Roman came were bittersweet. She wanted to be with Roman, especially since his visits were so infrequent, but when he took Isaiah out it allowed her to catch up on the work. She watched tutorial videos from her new laptop– Serena was slower with a computer than almost everybody her age, but she figured it out– and she relentlessly plodded through the worksheets and practice problems until Roman and Isaiah returned.

And then Roman brought them all out to dinner, and he teased her about ordering sparkling "wine" – she'd be twenty-one very soon, thank God– and over the meal he caught her up on everything going down in Florin. After dinner they walked along the riverside docks, Roman sometimes holding a drowsy Isaiah. They went back to the apartment after sundown and put Isaiah to bed. Then finally, finally, when they were alone...

"I'm gonna catch the biggest fish," Isaiah said. "It's gonna be the biggest fish anybody ever saw."

"Uh huh. Kiss me goodbye, Isie."

"Goodbye, Ma."

"Okay. Don't be out too late."

She watched the two of them rumble off in Roman's Pegasus, feeling both happy and tense.

She didn't know how to break the news to Roman. It felt wrong to let him take Isaiah out while she sat on this secret, but at least Isaiah could have one good afternoon with his idol before his Mama ruined everything.

Stay positive.

I am positive. Positively going to lose him.

She glanced up and saw Isaiah had left Dinosaur behind. *He's growing up.*

Serena focused on her work, drifting off into a trance that broke hours later when the sound of the Pegasus coming up the street interrupted the normal hum of distant traffic.

Serena's apartment sat in a quiet, tidy area of Rowanville. A mix of black and white folks lived here, and all seemed to be the type of people who minded their business.

She waited outside and watched Roman's truck round the corner. A cool autumn wind whirled leaves around her feet. *Calm*, Serena thought to her racing heart. *Calm.*

The Pegasus pulled up. Isaiah bounded out and came running at her full speed. "Ma! Ma, we're home!"

Serena had no more time to worry. Isaiah recounted the day in vivid detail, describing everything from the types of flowers they saw to the exact length of every fish they caught and what tackle he used and which tackle he hated because it stank. Isaiah caught a bluegill, and Roman a largemouth bass plus a pike as long as his forearm. Also, Mister Roman said they could go to a different spot next time and try his hand at catfishing.

"That's a little dangerous, Isaiah."

"It's not, Ma, because I'll be with Mister Roman."

"So if Mister Roman asked you to jump off a cliff, you'd do it?"

"Yes," said Isaiah.

She dressed the boy in a neat white shirt, blue dress pants and smart brown shoes. "You better not dirty these before we leave the house. We're going out to a nice dinner."

"You need to fix your hair, Ma. It's gettin' everywhere."

She pulled his nose and hurried for the master bathroom. Roman was just emerging from his own shower. She paused to admire him. Roman had lost some weight around his middle, but not much. His powerful frame still sent shivers up her back. So many nights she spent alone now just picturing that workman's body riding her hard into the bed, coming inside her.

"How do you get water on the *ceiling*?" Serena exclaimed as she prepared to shower. "It's like a tidal wave went through here."

"I was trying not to trip over the hundred million or so shampoo bottles," Roman replied dryly.

"Run along, Mister Roman. I got to get in."

"Mm." He caught her in the bathroom door and kissed her. His lips told hers just how much he'd missed her, too. She sighed and melted in his arms, tingling from the heat still coming off his bare skin. "I can't wait for tonight," he murmured, playing with the hem of her shirt.

"Mm. Me neither."

"I'm dying to fuck you right now."

"We can't," she whispered.

"What if we did it fast? Just turn around."

He placed her hand where he throbbed under the towel. Usually this worked on Serena. She kissed him hungrily, squeezed his cock hard enough to make him hiss, then darted into the bathroom, slamming the door shut.

That was close.

He pounded on the door. "Serena!"

"Dinner!" she reminded him, turning on the water.

"I'm taking you somewhere new tonight," he said, his voice muffled by the door and the running water. She missed his next words.

"Can you make sure Isaiah doesn't dirty up that shirt?" she hollered back.

Thinking ahead, she'd brought her change of clothes into the bathroom so he wouldn't see her naked body. Once she got clean and dry, she stepped into the flowy maxi dress that revealed absolutely zero underneath, and then piled up her hair into the pineapple bun.

"You alright?" he murmured as she walked out into the living room.

"Me? Yeah, I'm fine." *I'm freaking out.*

They took a different route, but of course Roman had mentioned they were trying something new. Apparently something out of the city? She frowned as he took the highway exit and the low-lying sprawl of Rowanville became just green hills and pasture.

Thirty minutes later they pulled up to the chosen venue: a winery.

Oh, my God.

"Um," she laughed nervously. "Roman, you know I'm too young to drink, right?"

He waved a hand. "I know the folks that run it. You can have whatever you want."

"Isaiah is a child."

Roman raised an eyebrow. "Oh, really? There I was, thinking he could drive us home after."

"It's not funny."

"Sarie, relax. There's a restaurant in there and he can get something for himself."

"I want wine," Isaiah said.

"No," said Roman and Serena at the same time.

The winery looked like the type of place that could swallow up a rent check in one meal. At her waitressing job Serena served a similar clientele. But this wasn't some cute little restaurant with booths and privacy where you could drop a big announcement on somebody and hurry out to the streets if things got crazy.

Tell him. Tell him now.

"I got something for you," Roman said, shutting off the engine. He glanced at the backseat, and Isaiah giggled. "The little man helped me pick it out."

"What is it?"

He dug in the pocket of his dress pants. Dress pants? Had he been wearing those when he left the house? And a *linen shirt*? He looked so good. And she hadn't noticed because she was too busy worrying about the fact that he was going to leave her.

Roman handed her something wrapped in delicate white tissue paper. "I was gonna get a box, but I wanted to surprise you and a box is hard to fit in there with all the extra equipment."

"Ha ha. What is this, Roman?" With shaking fingers she opened the tissue wrapper, twisted at both ends like the caramel candy she'd once sold to Mrs. Loving's church. The delicate jewelry nearly spilled into her lap. "Oh!"

She held it in her palm to inspect under the fading sunset light. A tiny gold orchid swung from a gold chain. A ruby winked in the center of the calyx like a shining red heart.

"Oh my goodness. Roman..."

"You like it?"

She nodded, fighting a sudden and very annoying surge of tears. "Will you put it on for me?"

He did, his big fingers managing the tiny clasp with surprising finesse. "I felt bad about losing the one you got me," he murmured. "As for this...well, you can't kill it, at least." He winced. "That sounds wrong. You know what I mean."

Tell him.

"I'll never take it off," she promised. "Thank you, Roman."

He tinkled the pendant with a long finger. She recognized the look on his face. He was about to ruin it.

Her heart leapt. "What?"

He had the nerve to look guilty. "Don't get mad. I didn't tell you, but this is a family dinner."

"*What*?"

"My brothers are here. Rebel and Ross. And Rebel's woman, too."

Serena stared ahead in horror. "I...how do I look?"

"You look like the woman of my dreams," he said, with surprising feeling. "You're one pretty girl, Serena, and you don't need pounds of makeup or a dress for that to be true. You're absolutely stunning and I say that for a fact. "

Isaiah groaned.

Roman took her hand and shook it gently. "Come on. Nothing to be scared of except Ross and Rebel maybe trying to kill each other. And you get to drink wine." He winked.

"Um, Roman. Actually—"

A deafening honk interrupted her. Isaiah clapped two hands over his ears. Roman glanced through his rear view and muttered, "Rebel."

A tall blonde man climbed out of a dusty red truck. On the passenger's side the woman from the grocery store, Minnie Brown, made a much more graceful landing. She gave Serena a friendly smile, and Roman a tight-lipped nod which he barely returned.

Ten minutes later, Serena sat in a full-body sweat opposite Minnie Brown and her apparent fiancé, Roman's younger brother. Ross was a no-show. Which was fine by Serena, since she much preferred the easygoing Rebel.

"So this is the girl who turned Florin on its head." Rebel smiled at her. "How is Rowanville treating you?"

"Um. It's fine. I like the city more than I thought I would."

The winery was beautiful. The dining happened on a circular stone terrace overlooking an expanse of rolling green gone dusky in the glow of sunset. Their table sat under a trellis overgrown with a purple trumpet vine. The centerpiece crystal bowl was filled with water, and the breeze pushed cut violet blossoms back and forth across its surface. They had not ordered yet. She touched the orchid pendant again and again, feeling sick to her stomach.

"I'm surprised you're not cold," Minnie told Serena, making conversation, since Serena was sitting there mute as a stump. "It's freezing up here."

"I don't get cold easily." *Living in old nasty trailers with no heat gives you a high tolerance.* Serena cleared her throat. "Um, so you're a vet, Minnie?"

"Yes, that's right. I just got out of school a couple years ago."

"I'm going to kindergarten in a week," Isaiah informed Rebel. "I'm going to kindergarten and Ma is going to get her GED. But I'm a little old for kindergarten just like Ma is too old for the diploma."

"Isaiah, baby, what do you want to eat?" Said Serena, tapping the menu. Her face flamed. Miss Minnie Brown, veterinarian, didn't need to hear about Serena getting a GED.

"I got my GED a couple years ago," Rebel said, surprising her. "Over a decade late, so I'd say you're right on time."

"I never bothered with that," Roman said. Then checked himself and added quickly for Isaiah's benefit, "But school is extremely important."

"Ma says she's going to college after the GED."

"What do you want to study, Serena?" asked Minnie politely.

"Um," said Serena. "Well, eventually, I'd like to be a nurse."

"Good evening, folks!"

All four of them jumped. A beaming waiter materialized at Roman's elbow. "What are we having tonight? Maybe we'll start off with a bottle for the table?" he boomed.

"I'm game," said Rebel, glancing round. "Minnie and I got a place at the villa so we're set."

Roman ruffled Isaiah's head. "You thinking you can drive us home, little man?"

"Yes," Isaiah said firmly.

Roman turned to the waiter. "I'll just have a glass of the *Leon*. Serena?" He frowned. "You alright?"

"Um," she said. "I won't be drinking tonight."

"Beg your pardon, Miss?" the waiter said brightly. "I couldn't catch that."

"I don't— I'm fine, thanks. No wine for me."

"What? Really?" Roman blinked. "Why not?"

"We have a great selection," the waiter leapt in, as if he'd spent his whole life longing to do so. "Every wine here is crafted of the highest quality vines from our Carolina vineyards. We have some award-winning vintages, but if you're in the mood for something more refreshing, perhaps the rosé -"

"Pregnant," said Rebel, slapping a hand on the table. "You're pregnant, aren't you?"

"*REBEL*," Minnie hissed. "What a thing to say!"

"What?" Growled Roman.

"What!" Shouted Isaiah.

"Oh my," the waiter said. "Oh my goodness. I had no idea, Miss, honest. It's just, you know, we don't get a lot of pregnant folks up here."

"Very funny, Rebel," said Roman, pissed. "She's not pregnant."

"Then why is she crying? Here, sugar." Rebel passed her his napkin. "It's alright." He looked sorry. "Shit. I didn't think that one through."

"No, you didn't," Minnie said, looking ready to strangle him. "Serena, are you okay?"

"Yes," she said. She dabbed at her watering eyes. She wasn't *crying*. She was just *tearing up*. "I'm fine." She refused to look at Roman.

"You know, we have a very nice creme brûlée for dessert," the waiter said helpfully. "That always cheers me right up, Miss. And don't worry, you can cry right into them napkins. People do it all the time."

"Friend," said Rebel, "Can you give us a minute?"

"Sure thing, sir. I'll be right back with that creme brûlée."

Roman still hadn't said anything. The touch on her thigh came from Isaiah. He looked...happy. His little face shone with it. He was the happiest boy in the world.

"Serena," Roman rasped. "Is it true?"

"Yes."

Roman got up from the table and walked out.

"Well," said Minnie into the brittle, ugly silence. "Tell us how you really feel."

Serena was numb. Just...numb.

"Y'all are wrong," said Rebel. "You didn't see his face. Go to him, Serena."

She shook her head. "There's no point."

"Go to him. Talk to him."

"I...I'll be fine." She put her hand on Isaiah's shoulder. Isaiah looked around, confused at the sudden change in mood.

Minnie leaned across the table and said passionately, "Don't worry, Serena. I'll help you with all I can. I know people who can help. My friend Chrissie is a nurse– she lives in Rowanville. She can get you appointments and checkups– I'll give you her number–"

"What did I miss?" said Ross, breezing up to the table, his jacket looped casually over his shoulder. "Why is Roman crying in the parking lot?"

The door of the Pegasus was open. One leg rested on the step, halfway outside. He put out the cigarette as she approached.

"Darling."

"Yeah."

"Darling, come here."

He came out of the truck and hugged her. They held each other.

"It's true? Really?"

"Yes."

"How long you known?"

"I'm three months along."

"You couldn't tell before?"

"I never had regular periods. I didn't start feeling bad until a couple weeks ago. It's not like it was with Isaiah, and I just knew from the jump." She took a breath to steady herself. "Do you want it, Roman?"

He laughed as if the question was crazy. "Yes. Yes, babe, I want it. I would love to have a child with you."

"I thought you were angry."

"I was about to goddamned break down in there. Thinking about Saverin. And Sam. And everybody else I hurt. Katie... She's gonna have a sibling she won't know. I'm happy but I just— it's eating me up to be happy. I'm not a good man. I don't want— hurt anybody else."

She tried to pull away as his voice cracked, but he held her still by force. "No. Don't look at me."

"Roman, it's gonna be fine."

"I can't lose you, Serena."

"Who says you're losing me? You mean to the baby?"

"No. Not the baby. I mean everything else. I want to always protect you."

"We'll do the best we can." She worked her arms loose from his death-grip and hugged Roman around his muscular waist. She rested her ear right in the middle of his warm, solid chest. He hugged her back. "I'm happy. Serena, I'm so damned happy," he said in a voice choked with more emotion than she'd ever heard Roman betray.

"We're gonna be a family," she whispered.

He cupped her face in his hands and kissed her. Sweet and slow.

Above them, from the terrace, Rebel gave a whoop. Roman flipped him the bird. “Ma!” Isaiah screamed. “Is it a boy or a girl?”

“Isaiah! Stop hollerin’ like I didn’t raise you.” But she laughed as she wiped her eyes.

“Your creme brûlée is here,” said Ross. “If you don’t eat it I just might.”

Snorting, Roman opened the door of the Pegasus to screen her from view. Just the two of them now.

“Serena, would you marry me?”

Her face gleamed with light and love. “Yes,” she said in stunned, happy surprise. “I will.”

CHAPTER 16
EPILOGUE II

Roman picked up the phone on the tenth ring, lowering his voice so he wouldn't wake Serena.

"What?"

"Roman?" Rain's voice sounded muffled, like he was getting over a cold. "Roman, is that you?"

"Yeah, it's me."

"Um." *Sniff*. "Roman, I need your help."

"I'm not giving you money, Rain." In the darkness Roman found Serena's hip and stroked it. "I'm done with that. Either you get clean, or you fuck off."

"Brother...I just need you right now. I need you to come get me. It hurts so bad."

"What hurts?"

"Everything. Everywhere. I need you to come get me."

Not this shit again.

“Where are you?” Roman said gruffly.

“In the back hills,” Rain replied. “I took something and I think I’m fucked up.”

“Call an ambulance.”

“You’re my brother. You have to help me. We look out for each other, don’t we? Roman, I’m begging you. This is the last time.”

Roman shut his eyes. He thought of his warm bed. His soon-to-be wife sleeping beside him. His stepson in the other room. All the shit he had to take care of tomorrow to make sure the mountain was safe for Serena and Isaiah to return to. Not to mention the search for Katie, which was going nowhere.

“I’m busy,” he said.

“Fuck you,” Rain roared, the pleading tone disappearing. “FUCK YOU! Go to hell, you fucking bastard whoreson! You ain’t no brother to me. You’re dead to me! DEAD!”

Junkie rage. Roman hung up. He turned over in bed and pulled Serena close, forcing back his own anger. He focused on his beautiful Serena, on the future mother of his child, on everything he’d built. His life stood on shaky ground, though he felt the happiest he’d ever been.

If he started letting Rain back into his life, he’d put his newfound happiness with Serena and her boy in danger. Serena was pregnant. He couldn’t have a fucking junkie around his kid.

And it wasn’t like he never helped Rain before. Money, places to stay, checking him into rehab. The fact of the matter was that Rain just wanted to throw his life away. Well, let him. Roman was done wading through shit to retrieve it.

“Baby?” Serena mumbled. “Who was that?”

“Rain.”

“Oh. Is he in trouble?”

“Probably not.”

“You gonna check on him?”

“No. Go to sleep, Serena.”

“Mmm.” She snuggled closer. He curled his arms around her protectively, stroking her back.

He thought of Saverin.

He thought of Sam.

“Baby?”

“Yeah?”

“You’re thinking real loud in my ears.” Her eyes drifted open. She was so lovely, sometimes he couldn’t believe it. “You should go check on him,” she mumbled, stroking his chest.

“I know.” He kissed her, sweet and slow, until she was warm and soft and shuddering in his arms. He slid two fingers inside her, thrusting slowly a few times before he withdrew. “I’ll be back soon, love.”

“Be careful.”

“It’ll be fast. Go to sleep.”

"Mmm...love you." She drifted off.

Roman got dressed and called the number back.

Rain answered immediately. The change in his voice sent chills up Roman's neck. He sounded hopeful as a child at Christmas. "Roman?"

"Where are you, Rain?"

"Back hills. The hangman's tree. Hurry..."

Rain McCall hung up the phone and threw it into the dirt. He curled up on himself. He'd never felt so shitty in his life. His body felt like it was on fire, covered in scorpions, and at the same time, fucking frozen. But that would end. Soon. Very soon. Once he got the pills.

"Here you go," sneered Curley McCall, pushing the baggie towards him with his cane. "All yours, just like I said."

Rain picked up the bag with shaking hands. He avoided looking at Curley. While the Snatch Hill McCall would have never won a beauty contest in his prime, now he looked like an old, tough steak left too long on the edge of a grill. Curley's face was scarred with burns like Saverin Bailey's, but half the hair on his head would never grow back. He'd jumped from Roman's top floor and landed badly. Fucked up his leg, so now he walked with a cane. They'd taken him to the hospital in Rowanville, but he'd broken out and was now hiding out in the back hills, avoiding Roman's vengeance until Rain placed this golden opportunity straight into his lap.

"You gonna kill him?" Rain mumbled, opening the baggie almost reverently. He should feel bad for Roman. He should feel guilty. Sick to his stomach. But all he wanted was to get high.

Rain poured the contents of the baggie into his palm and crushed the whole lot between his teeth. He swallowed without tasting.

"There," Curley chuckled. "Ain't that better?"

"Yeah," Rain sighed. He didn't feel anything. Just...bliss.

Empty white bliss.

He waited with Curley and the other Snatch Hills, high as a fucking kite. Somewhere in the distance Roman was coming loyally to his rescue. Walking right into the trap.

As Rain had known he would.

Judas.

"Shoot me," he said to Curley in a voice as empty as he felt. "Shoot me before he gets here. I can't look at him."

"No," said Curley, gesturing to his men to prepare. "I want you to watch."

To be continued....

SMALL TOWN

ROGUE

BOOK THREE

MARION MEADOWS

AFTERWORD

The next book in the BWWM Small Town Saga will be *Small Town Rogue.* It will pick up after the events of *Small Town King.*

CONTINUE THE STORY...

CONTINUE THE STORY...

Chrissie Harper is tired. She's tired of low-value men and getting jumped by angry baby mamas. She's tired of dates at Denny's. So at first, Rain McCall seemed like a dream come true. Cute. Polite. Funny. Rich. A big you-know-what. Before she knows it, Chrissie's in love. But this man of her dreams has an ugly secret. Forced to choose herself, Chrissie checks into the Heartbreak Hotel and promises to forget Rain forever. Now he's back. And he won't take no for an answer... Even if its her wedding day?!

Made in the USA
Middletown, DE
10 January 2023

21775171R00165